"I'm so sorry for

"You've said that before and I get it. But I'm not going back." He'd believed she'd be in his life forever. But then she'd walked away.

"I can't undo what I did last year." She touched her belly. "I can't undo this. I also can't give this baby up. She's mine and I won't let her down, even though I seem to be letting everyone else down these days."

"That's the most important thing, Grace. Be there for him, and if you do that, you've done everything right."

"She," Grace said as she walked away. "My baby is a girl."

"Nope, that's a boy you're carrying, Grace Thomas. I'll eat my hat if it isn't," he called out after her.

The thinnest laugh carried back to him as she walked into the department store. He watched her go, thinking back to when he'd first met her. She'd had it all, but she'd wanted to spend a year being a cowgirl.

He'd loved her fearlessness. And then he'd just plain loved her.

He still loved her, but he was determined not to let it show.

Brenda Minton lives in the Ozarks with her husband, children, cats, dogs and strays. She is a pastor's wife, Sunday school teacher, coffee addict and sleep deprived. Not in that order. Her dream to be an author for Harlequin started somewhere in the pages of a romance novel about a young American woman stranded in a Spanish castle. Her dreams came true, and twenty-plus books later, she is an author hoping to inspire young girls to dream.

Books by Brenda Minton

Love Inspired

Martin's Crossing

A Rancher for Christmas
The Rancher Takes a Bride
The Rancher's Second Chance

Cooper Creek

Christmas Gifts
"Her Christmas Cowboy"
The Cowboy's Holiday Blessing
The Bull Rider's Baby
The Rancher's Secret Wife
The Cowboy's Healing Ways
The Cowboy Lawman
The Cowboy's Christmas Courtship
The Cowboy's Reunited Family
Single Dad Cowboy

Visit the Author Profile page at Harlequin.com for more titles.

The Rancher's Second Chance

Brenda Minton

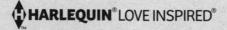

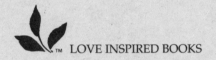 LOVE INSPIRED BOOKS

Recycling programs
for this product may
not exist in your area.

ISBN-13: 978-0-373-87979-3

The Rancher's Second Chance

Copyright © 2015 by Brenda Minton

www.Harlequin.com

Printed in U.S.A.

And not only *that*, but we also glory in tribulations, knowing that tribulation produces perseverance; and perseverance, character; and character, hope.
—*Romans* 5:3–4

To the readers, for your many prayers
and messages of encouragement.
The best journey is a journey with friends.

To Melissa Endlich.
I hope you know how much I appreciate you,
your insight, your encouragement.

Chapter One

The pounding on the front door roused Brody Martin from the deepest, most pain-free sleep he'd had in a good long while. He groaned, covering his face with his arm. No way was he going to the door. No way in the world was he waking up to go work cattle with Duke, his older brother, when it was miserable and pouring down rain outside.

He'd prefer dry and miserable inside to wet and miserable outside. It wasn't worth it. Ask his joints, they'd agree. At one month short of twenty-seven he felt as if those cattle they worked had trampled all over him.

Whoever had been at the door had stopped pounding, and he closed his eyes, ready to go back to sleep. The next thing he knew someone was outside his window yelling at him to wake up. When a hand hit the window, the dog came out from under the blankets, barking, ready to defend Brody and the house. Brody pulled the dog back and ordered it to hush. The white mop bared its teeth and crouched next to him.

"Brody, you've got to let me in. He's going to kill me."

It was a female voice, muffled through the glass, but obviously in distress.

No self-respecting man could ignore a statement like that. He shot out of bed and hurried as fast as his overused knees could take him to the front door. The dog raced ahead, barking. When he yanked open the door, the woman standing on the front step of the trailer, shivering in the cold rain, fell into the house.

She was on her knees, sobbing, and Brody didn't quite know what to do with her. Or if he wanted anything to do with her now that he knew who had woken him from a sound sleep. He pulled the door closed, gathering up sympathy as he did. He really wasn't a heartless cur. He just protected his heart a little better these days.

He managed to get down on the floor next to her, pushing aside the crazy white mop of a dog that crouched on its belly, licking her hand. When he lifted her face to get a good look, he let out a few words that would have gotten his mouth washed out with soap not too many years back. A purple mark on her cheek and a black eye marred her pale skin. Tears streamed down her cheeks. He'd known it wouldn't be good for her when she'd left him for Lincoln. He hadn't expected it to be this bad.

He pulled her close, gently touching the dark marks that marred her pretty face. He brushed short blond hair back from her eyes and waited. He might not be good for much, but he was good at waiting.

It took her a few minutes to calm down. As he stroked her hair, her breathing returned to normal and the tears dried.

"Lincoln?" he asked as she pulled away, brushing

a hand across her eyes to dry the last of her tears. Lincoln Carter, his once-upon-a-time roommate, best friend and traveling partner. And the man who couldn't keep his hands off another man's woman.

Grace Thomas. Until last year, she'd been the woman Brody thought he might marry. Then less than a week after she'd broken things off with him, she'd been seen stepping out with Lincoln.

A real man didn't do that to a friend. But then a real man didn't hit a woman, either. That was a mighty big strike against Lincoln Carter.

"Grace?"

"I knew his temper was bad. I shouldn't have..."

"Don't make excuses for him." Brody shook his head, thinking he'd heard it all when one of the toughest females he knew had found herself in a situation such as this and then tried to let the man off the hook with an excuse. It just went to prove that it could happen to anyone. Grace had a college degree, an educated and respectable family and backbone.

Lincoln could manipulate a snake out of its skin and make the serpent believe it was being done a favor.

"I'm not making excuses," Grace sobbed. "I just knew and I shouldn't have pushed. I shouldn't have..."

"I keep hearing you say you shouldn't have, but what about him, Grace? What about this?" He touched her cheek, barely making contact with the bruise, yet she still flinched. Her dark brown eyes flickered with pain and she looked away.

"I know." Her voice trembled on the acknowledgment.

"He shouldn't have touched you, and I'll make him sorry..."

He shook off the threat. It wasn't his place. Instead, he reached for the coffee table and pushed himself to his feet, grimacing at the pain that shot through his knees.

He extended a hand to the woman kneeling on his floor and she took it, allowing him to help her up. She was a tiny thing, a tough-as-nails cowgirl. She had a lot of sense, except when it came to Lincoln. He still couldn't figure out why or how she'd gotten tangled up with the other man.

"I'm not making excuses anymore, Brody."

He didn't say anything, just led her to the kitchen that connected to the living room of his trailer. He pulled a bag of corn out of the freezer and handed it to her. She thanked him quietly and held it to her eye and cheek.

Because he didn't know what else to do, he started a pot of coffee, then took eggs out of the fridge. A quick look inside the appliance and he also found bacon.

"Are you hungry?"

She nodded. She'd taken a seat at the bistro-style table that he'd bought because it fit the small space in the single-wide mobile home. The trailer was his personal space on the Circle M Ranch, a ranch that had been in the Martin family for more than a hundred years.

He'd had the trailer set on a foundation a good walk from the barn and from either of his brothers. He wanted to be here, but he didn't want to be under their thumbs. Because Duke and Jake had helped to raise him after their mom skipped out on them some twenty years ago, they thought they still had the right to tell him how to live his life.

They didn't get that he needed space.

He'd really hoped once Jake married Breezy and got down to the business of raising the orphaned twin nieces they shared, and had a baby of his own on the way, he would be too busy to involve himself in Brody's life. It hadn't worked out that way. Now both Jake and his wife, Breezy, were in Brody's business. And then came Duke and his soon-to-be wife, Oregon. He couldn't forget their daughter, Lilly. Thinking of his precocious twelve-year-old niece, Brody had to smile. Family wasn't all bad. It just meant not having a lot of time to himself.

If his sister, Samantha, would come home, she could pull some outrageous stunt and get them all off his back.

Brody found a skillet and placed it on the back burner of the stove. He started frying the bacon and then he cracked a few eggs in a bowl, stirred in a little milk and a handful of cheese. He couldn't cook much, but he could make decent bacon and scrambled eggs. Toast wasn't too far out of his league, either.

"When did it start?" he asked the woman sitting at the table.

"Almost from the beginning. At first it wasn't like this. A bruise on my arm or wrist, grabbing me a little too tightly. He was careful that Aunt Jacki didn't see."

He nodded, because he didn't know what to say. Grace had been living with her aunt Jacki when he met her. It had been her summer to find herself, she'd told him. Jacki Thomas had helped her do that, he guessed. As far as he could tell, Jacki was the black sheep of the upstanding Thomas family.

"And you thought he was someone you wanted to

keep dating?" Brody couldn't help but ask, knowing it sounded more like a snarl than a civilized question.

When she didn't answer, he chanced a look at her. She wiped at her eyes and nodded. "Oh, Brody, I'm so sorry."

Not much he could say to that, so he shrugged and went back to cooking. If he spent too much time looking at her, he'd get all stupid and heartsick again. He'd start thinking about that ring he'd never given her. Start remembering all the dreams he'd had for the two of them. That had been his mistake, making plans when she hadn't been interested in anything long-term. Not with him anyway.

Young and stupid. Yep, that description fit him perfectly. If he gave her a chance, no doubt she'd apologize. Make excuses for why she'd left him. And he'd let her off the hook. The bacon sizzled in the pan, the aroma waking him up a little. He poured two cups of coffee and set one in front of her.

"Have you called your folks?" he asked as he headed back to the skillet and the bacon.

"No. They're out of the country. They're on a medical mission trip in South America for the next year."

He kept his back to her, his attention focused on the pan. "What about your grandparents? Or Aunt Jacki?"

"Aunt Jacki went to Florida for a few months. I didn't want to be there alone when Lincoln came looking for me. And my grandparents went to Africa for a month with a group from their church."

"What do you want from me, Grace?"

She didn't answer. When he turned away from the stove she was staring at the floor, her shoulders slumped forward. The dog had managed to get her attention and now slept in her lap. Brody's heart caved a little.

He had a hard time being strong around women, especially this woman. And weak was the last thing he needed to be when it came to Grace Thomas.

"Grace, I can't help you if I don't know what you want."

"I need a place to stay. Somewhere he can't find me. I tried breaking up with him a few months ago but he keeps calling. He won't stay away from Jacki's." Her eyes closed and tears slid down her cheeks.

"He isn't going to come after you, is he? You're gone and he's probably feeling fortunate that you didn't press charges."

"I did press charges. He's in jail. And when he gets out he'll be furious."

Brody smiled, imagining his old friend in the slammer. "Well, that ought to teach him. Good for you, Gracie."

"You haven't called me that in a long time."

"Yeah, well, it didn't seem right to call you that once you decided to leave me for my best friend."

He fixed her a plate of cheesy scrambled eggs and bacon. When he put the plate in front of her she turned green, covered her mouth with her hand and ran down the hall to the bathroom.

He had a real bad feeling.

The nausea eased, and Grace leaned back against the closed door of the bathroom. Stupid. Stupid. Stupid. She had made some bad choices in her life, really bad choices. But Lincoln had been the worst ever. She didn't know how she'd become this person, forgetting herself, what she wanted out of life and who she had always known herself to be. She'd lost her way. That was what her granddad would say. Her life had been easy, smooth sailing. And then Lincoln had ensnared her.

A light rap vibrated the door. "You okay in there?"

"Oh, yeah. Wonderful." She stood and turned on cold water to splash her face. He knocked again. She reached for a towel, wiped away the dampness, then stood there with the towel against her cheeks looking at the stranger in the mirror. A stranger with her eyes but with marks left by a man who had no right to do this, to take the best part of her and turn her into someone she no longer recognized.

She shouldn't have stayed in the relationship. She should have walked away the first time. If anyone had asked her a year ago if she'd ever let a man hit her, she would have told them she'd make sure he regretted it if he tried. But Lincoln had hit her. More than once.

For a while she'd stayed in the relationship because Lincoln had a way of convincing her he loved her and that she could change him. And then she'd stayed because she'd been afraid to leave. He'd convinced her that the abuse was her fault and that she needed to change.

When she finally had walked away, he hadn't been willing to end things. Tonight she'd made the mistake of opening the door and he'd pushed his way in.

She was going to find herself again. Calling the police had been the first step in that process.

"Want me to feed the eggs to the dog?" Brody asked through the paper-thin door. She could imagine him out there, forehead against the door, hand on the knob.

"No, I'm good. Please don't let the dog have my breakfast."

She opened the door, trying hard to avoid looking at the man standing there so casually, leaning against the wood-paneled wall. While his stance said *casual*, he would never fit that description. At six feet with blue eyes that tripped a girl up and dark hair that she knew to be soft beneath her fingers, Brody Martin could be lethal. His cowboy charm fooled a girl. No, he fooled a lot of people with that good-ole-boy act.

He shifted away from the wall and his steady gaze held her in place. She looked away at first, her hand going to her cheek. Feather soft his hand touched her arm. She flinched but didn't mean to.

"You okay?"

She nodded but couldn't form the words to assure him. If she spoke out loud, she'd cry. If he said anything, she'd cry harder. If he touched her, the dam would definitely break, and she'd probably never be able to get control again.

He gave her a long look and kept his distance.

"Let's eat before that mutt gets our eggs. She loves 'em." He motioned her to walk ahead of him.

She poured herself a fresh cup of the coffee. Now that her stomach had settled, she thought she could keep it down. She needed it. She'd been awake all night. Through the kitchen window she could see that it was morning now. Not a sunny morning, but dreary like the night that had just passed. The world was gray and a steady rain fell.

Brody walked up behind her. He took a plate off the counter and handed it to her. She watched him limp to the fridge. He didn't say anything. He pulled out a jar of salsa and limped back to the table.

"Your knee isn't better?" she asked him as she sat.

He sat across from her. "Nope."

"You've been like that since the surgery or before. You're worse now than you were when…"

He looked up, his blue eyes accusing. She glanced away, unsure how to continue.

"Yeah, there are a lot of ways I'm worse off than I was then. Thanks."

"I didn't leave you for Lincoln." She at least owed him that explanation.

"You broke up with me, and the next week you were with Lincoln."

"I know." She closed her eyes, thinking back to all that had come between them. Her fears of getting too serious when her time in Stephenville was limited. His overwhelming need to keep her close. She hadn't been ready for his kind of serious.

She took a bite of egg. The dog came to sit on the floor next to her. The white bit of fluff stood on its hind legs and begged. She tossed it a piece of egg.

"Where did you get the dog?" she asked, hoping to ease the tension between them. "A Maltese? She isn't really the kind of dog I pictured a bull-riding cowboy to have."

"I'm not a bull rider anymore. I'm just a guy living on a ranch, running some cattle with my brothers."

"Oh." She didn't know what else to say. She knew he'd wanted to be a world champion. She knew about dreams and how they drove a person. She'd dreamed of seeing a little more of the country before settling down into the rest of her life.

He'd had other dreams he'd shared with her. He'd wanted to find the mother who'd walked out on them. He didn't want to be a man who gave up the way his dad had. He rarely talked about how his mom's abandonment had affected him, but it was there, not so far beneath the surface. He had a hard time trusting.

He cleared his throat and tossed the dog a piece of bacon.

"I got the dog at the grocery store in Austin. She was thin and her hair was matted. The guy who had her wanted twenty bucks. I couldn't leave her." It was easier for him to talk about the dog than about bull riding.

That unwillingness to leave a stray was why she'd come here. Because as hard as he tried to be coldhearted, he wasn't. He couldn't leave behind a stray. He would never leave a friend to suffer.

"Brody, for what it's worth, I am sorry."

"I'm sure you are." He gave her a pointed look, his gaze lingering on her bruised face.

"I'll go. After I eat, I'll leave."

He slid his plate to the side. "Where would you go, Grace? Your parents are out of the country. What's your plan?"

She shrugged, aching inside because she didn't have a plan. She'd taken off in the middle of the night knowing she needed to put miles between herself and Lincoln. She hadn't really planned on coming here. But when she'd put her car in gear, she'd found herself on the road to Martin's Crossing.

"We'll figure something out."

With that he got up, cleared the plates and fed the scraps to the dog that was dancing around the kitchen.

On hind legs, her toenails painted pink and a bow pinned between her ears, she was the last dog on earth Grace would ever expect Brody Martin to own.

For a long while Brody busied himself at the sink washing dishes. He kept his back to her, his attention focused on the plates he washed and the window over the sink. He probably expected Lincoln to show up anytime. But she'd taken the battery out of his truck, so it would take him a while.

A second wave of nausea hit, taking her by surprise. Grace ran for the bathroom and this time she didn't shut the door. As she lost her breakfast, Brody appeared at her side. He didn't say anything. A moment later she heard water running, then felt a cool cloth settle over the back of her neck.

Brody's hand rested on her shoulder. He didn't stay at her side, though. She heard his booted footsteps going down the hall, away from her. She pulled the cloth off her neck and wiped her face free of tears.

When she returned to the kitchen he was sitting at the table, his leg propped up on the empty chair. He had a cup of coffee in his hands and the dog on his lap.

"So how far along are you?" His gaze brushed down her body, lingering on the loose button-up shirt she'd pulled on over her T-shirt.

Grace leaned against the counter and tried to shift her focus from his face, from the disappointment she would see. Emotions clogged her throat, making it hard to speak. She rubbed hands down cheeks that felt warm and took a deep breath.

"About four months," she admitted, shifting her

focus from the living room with worn leather furniture to the man sitting in front of her.

"I see." Brody brushed a hand through his dark hair. "I guess he knows and isn't too happy?"

"No, he isn't." It hurt too much to think about the clinic Lincoln had driven her to in another state. They'd sat in the parking lot for an hour as he'd tried to talk her in to making a choice she didn't want to make. In the end she'd refused. He'd been angry, but he hadn't seen a way to force her into the building.

She'd ended their relationship that day. But Lincoln kept coming back.

"We need to find you a place to stay."

Because he wouldn't let her stay with him. That went without saying. "Brody, I hope someday you'll forgive me."

"Me, too." He said it so quietly that she had to lean in to catch the words. He limped to the living room and grabbed keys and his cell phone off the table. "Let's go."

On the way out the door he grabbed his hat, shoving it down tight on his head.

She followed him out the door to his truck. Rain was still coming down, heavy and cool. He opened the passenger side door for her and she slid in. Without asking he reached for the seat belt and pulled it across her lap. As if she was five years old and couldn't do it for herself.

The movement put them too close, and that was the last thing either of them needed. "I can do it, Brody."

"Yeah, I guess you can."

She clicked the seat belt in place and reached to close the door. Just then, a truck came up the drive and parked. Brody limped to the vehicle and his brother Jake got out. The other man studied her for a moment, then resumed his conversation with Brody. She'd met Brody's brothers a time or two at different events. She doubted they knew much about her, other than her name.

The two men continued to talk, acting as if they didn't notice the rain that soaked their clothes, dripped off their hats.

Jake Martin said something else to Brody. Brody raised a hand in a wave that became a salute. Grace knew the brothers were close. They'd raised each other and saved this ranch together. She also knew that having two older brothers sometimes got under Brody's skin.

Finally, he joined her in the truck, grumbling about older brothers who should stay out of his business. He jerked off his hat, tossed it in the backseat of his truck and brushed a hand through damp hair that formed loose curls. The tan skin of his face, stretched taught over lean cheeks and a strong jawline, was damp. He raised his arm and used his sleeve to wipe away the moisture.

"I don't want to cause you problems with your brothers."

"You aren't causing me any problems. They can't think of me as an adult."

She knew better. "No, they can't stand to see you hurt by the woman who cheated on you."

"They don't know about you. About us." He started the truck and eased out of the driveway. "I think I know where you can stay."

He didn't expand on that. Details weren't Brody's thing. She'd just have to trust him. Who else did she have?

And right now she had someone pretty tiny trusting her to make the right choices for them both.

Chapter Two

They drove to town in the pouring rain he'd wanted to avoid. The wipers swished in a continuous effort to keep the windshield clear. Brody slid a quick glance at the woman sitting next to him. She'd been quiet since leaving the ranch. Now he knew why. She'd fallen sound asleep, her hand on her slightly rounded belly.

He shook his head, trying not to think of the baby or the bruises on her face. The first made him a little queasy. The second made him so angry he couldn't see straight.

Even after what she'd done to him, he still cared. That made him a little bit mad at her, a lot mad at himself. He could help her out. He could forgive. But he wasn't going to let himself get tangled up with her again.

It didn't take long to reach their destination. Brody pulled to a stop in front of Oregon's All Things shop. Across the street at Duke's No Bar and Grill the lights were on and the open sign was lit up. A handful of cars and trucks were parked out front, people getting an early start on their day with breakfast at his older brother's restaurant.

After a few minutes the front door of the diner opened. Duke, tall and imposing and a little scary if a guy didn't know him, stepped out on the front porch. He greeted the few people who were brave enough to sit outside under the awning on a rainy morning. When he saw Brody he nodded and headed down the steps.

Brody got out of the truck and met his brother on the sidewalk in front of Oregon's. Duke and Oregon were going to be married in December. She was living in a cottage on the ranch while Duke completed remodeling the old farm house that had belonged to their grandfather. Their daughter, Lilly, bounced from house to house, wanting to spend time with both of them.

"What's going on?" Duke peered in the tinted windows of the truck. "Is that Grace Thomas?"

"Yeah." Brody held out his hand for the keys Duke had in his hand.

"Not so quick, little brother." Duke took a step closer to the truck. "What happened?"

"Lincoln." The one word brought anger to the surface all over again.

"Is that why you came home last year?" Duke tossed the keys in the air, then caught them. He didn't take his eyes off Brody. Brody did his best not to squirm.

"Part of the reason. She needs a place to stay."

"Somewhere that Lincoln can't find her?"

"Yeah, I guess. I don't think he'd bother looking here." Brody didn't want to waste time discussing it. He wanted to haul her into Oregon's, then get back to the ranch and get to work. For the first time in a long while he'd prefer Jake to Duke. He'd prefer all day in the saddle to five minutes alone with Grace.

"I don't know if I want you putting Lilly and Oregon in danger."

"Duke, she doesn't have anywhere else to go."

"Yeah, I get that. But Lincoln is going to come looking for her, isn't he?"

"Yeah, I reckon, but he won't think to look here. He'll come to my place."

Duke headed up the sidewalk with the key. "Brody, you can't save the whole world."

He didn't want to save the whole world. But saving Grace was something he had to do. He couldn't turn her away. He couldn't pretend he didn't care.

"Doesn't she have family she can turn to?" Duke asked as he unlocked the back door of Oregon's, which led to the small apartment at the rear of the shop.

"They're all out-of-pocket right now. Parents and grandparents are in the mission field and her aunt is in Florida."

"Gotcha." Duke flipped on lights and turned on the air conditioner. "I hate to ask, but are you sure you want to do this?"

"I don't have a choice." But if he was being honest with himself, getting tied in with Grace was the last thing he wanted.

"Right, okay." Duke didn't question him further. He went upstairs and came back with a blanket and a pillow. "I'd put her on the sofa for now."

Brody agreed. He walked out the door and down the sidewalk to his truck. She was still sleeping. She'd pulled her legs up in the seat and her arms hugged her waist. He opened the door and said her name. She murmured something soft that ended on a sigh.

"Great." He shook his head and reached in to wake her. She leaned toward him, her eyes still closed. Brody slid an arm around her shoulders and another under her legs. There wasn't much to her. He pulled her against him and stepped out of the truck, holding her tight as he made his way back up the sidewalk.

Blond hair lifted in the breeze and brushed his face. He inhaled the sweet apple scent of her shampoo. She smelled good. And she was easy to hold.

But he'd do himself some favors by remembering who she was, what she had done to him. Duke had the door open as Brody made his way back to the apartment. He shot a big-brother look at the woman in Brody's arms and then noticed the left leg that Brody couldn't quite manage to lift. Duke shook his head but didn't say anything.

Brody eased the sleeping woman to the sofa and covered her with the blanket. She curled on her side and her hand reached out. He stepped back away from her. A good five feet between them made him feel a lot better.

"Well, that looks like one hundred pounds of serious trouble," Duke chuckled. He pounded Brody on the back. "Go with God, little brother. I wouldn't want to be in your shoes."

"Thanks." Brody sat down in the easy chair and propped his booted feet up on the coffee table. He ignored the warning look Duke gave him.

"What are you going to tell Lincoln when he comes looking for her?" Duke leaned against the door frame.

He glanced out, toward the restaurant, then back at Brody.

"I guess I'll tell him she doesn't want to see him."

"Well, call if you need anything." And by anything, he meant help handling Lincoln Carter.

Hard to believe he and Lincoln once had been best friends. They'd both been working toward the same goal: to be world-champion bull riders. They'd won a lot of money. They'd traveled the country together. Last fall it all had changed. One year ago, Brody realized.

"Thanks for the help, Duke. I appreciate it." Brody tipped up his hat, making steady eye contact with his brother, who still stood in the doorway watching him.

"That's what family is for. I'd best get back to the breakfast crowd or Ned is going to hunt me down."

Brody smiled. Ned, short for Nedine, was a big lady with graying auburn hair and a gruff demeanor, but she was all heart. Duke said she was the best waitress in the state. He told her that often. Especially after he'd ruffled her feathers.

Duke left, and Brody leaned back in the chair and tried to relax. Unfortunately he was all too aware of the woman just feet away from him. Aware of her soft breathing. The quiet sob in her sleep. It all pulled him toward her in a way he hadn't expected and didn't want. He just should have called the police when she'd shown up. He should send her to friends. There were other people she could have gone to.

So why him?

To torment him, he guessed. The only one who could control that was him. He would take control now before he got too far in. He'd keep her at a distance. He'd remember how it felt to have his heart trampled. Memories resurfaced, and not the ones he wanted. Of course he didn't remember the night when he'd rounded the corner of his trailer and saw her with Lincoln. Instead, he remembered how it had felt to hold her in his arms.

He rubbed his hands down his cheeks and shook his head. Heartache, pain, disillusionment—he drew all the memories in and let them simmer as he looked at the woman asleep on the couch, her face bruised by the fist of another man.

He waited until he heard Oregon show up, then he made his way into the section of the building where her store was located. Oregon had a talent for making things. She made clothes, hand-painted Christmas ornaments and jewelry. He didn't know much about her art, but he knew enough to be impressed.

When he walked through the door, she turned from the shelf she was straightening and smiled at him. She was a tiny thing with dark hair and big gray eyes. And her daughter, Lilly, was the spitting image of Duke.

"I heard I have a visitor." She moved some things around, then settled her serious gaze on him. "You okay?"

"I'm good. She isn't. Do you mind if she stays here for a while?"

"Of course not." Oregon pointed to the coffeepot on the shelf behind the counter. "Need a cup?"

"No, I thought I'd go help Jake."

She narrowed her eyes to study him. "Really?"

"What?"

"You've avoided horses like most people avoid snakes."

He shrugged and didn't offer explanations. He hadn't offered an explanation to anyone about anything. He'd lived his life that way, because from the time he'd been a kid everyone had told him to put on his big-boy jeans and get over it. He'd gotten over his mom walking out on them. He'd gotten over his dad drinking his life away. And whatever he was feeling inside, he kept it to himself. For the most part.

As Duke had told him a long time ago, they all had stuff they had to deal with.

"He asked me to help him out today. I know Duke is at the restaurant. I don't want to leave Jake short-handed."

She dropped her gaze to his leg the way Duke had. "Should you be riding?"

"Yep. So can you let her know where I've gone?"

"Yes, I'll let her know."

Brody started to walk away but stopped. "If a guy with straw-colored hair and a big grin shows up here asking for her, tell him you don't know who he's talking about."

Worry clouded her features. "I will. Brody, are you sure you should…"

"Yeah, I should."

He walked away before she could guess he wasn't as sure as he acted.

Lincoln chased her through the dark, his face a mask of anger and cruelty. Grace ran but her legs were tired and heavy, and it was hard to breathe. Then suddenly they were in a clinic, and Lincoln told her in quiet, reassuring tones that it was the right choice. She shook her head, knowing he was wrong and that she couldn't do this. She couldn't take the life growing inside her. It was her baby. Hers to love. Hers to protect.

Grace woke up with a start. She wasn't in a clinic. She was—she didn't know where she was. Somewhere in the back of her mind she remembered being picked up from Brody's truck, his arms around her. It was the first time she'd felt safe in months.

It was true. A person always wanted what they knew they couldn't have. She happened to be the poster child for that. She hadn't wanted Brody when she'd dated him because she'd thought it was all moving too fast, getting too serious too soon. She'd wanted freedom and excitement before she had to go home and get back to reality.

In the past few months her reality had shifted, changed to the point she no longer knew what her future held or how to get back to the person she was or the person she'd always thought she'd be.

She pulled the blanket close as she studied the room. It was a tiny apartment, not much bigger than the bedroom she'd had growing up. The sofa she'd slept on and an overstuffed chair were the only furnishings. The small kitchen area was just a counter with a narrow stove, single sink and a dorm-size fridge. Stairs behind the sofa led to a loft.

The inside door opened and a woman with dark hair peeked in, saw that she was awake and entered the room with a smile. She held up a glass coffeepot. "You're awake. Need coffee?"

Grace shook her head, still holding the blanket tight. "No, thank you. I'm trying to cut back."

Because she was having a baby. Her heart clenched and she wanted to cry all over again. She drew in a deep breath and managed to smile so the woman in front of her wouldn't think she was falling apart.

The woman sat on the arm of the chair and set the coffeepot down on a magazine on the table. She studied Grace, her smile kind. "You'll make it through this."

Grace wanted to ask if this stranger could promise that. Instead, she managed a smile. "I hope so."

"You will. And you'll learn a lot about yourself. By the way, I'm Oregon Jeffries. I'm engaged to Brody's brother Duke."

"Grace Thomas. But you probably already know that."

"Brody did tell me your name. But he didn't tell me anything else. He keeps things to himself."

Grace nodded. Yes, that was the Brody she knew. She thought about how she used to try to get him to share gossip about people they met. But he never would. Instead, he'd told her everyone had a story and most didn't need to be repeated. Brody had his anger, his past, but he also had faith. He had convictions. The whole package that was Brody Martin had scared her a little. Oregon cleared her throat, bringing Grace back to the present.

"Sorry, I got lost in thought." Grace said. "Is it going to cause you problems, having me here? I wouldn't want to put you in danger."

"Of course you're not a problem. As for danger, Duke is right across the street."

"Thank you." Grace looked around the tiny room. She felt safe here.

"Is there anything at all I can get you?"

Grace thought about all of the possible answers to

that question. If only this woman, Oregon, could get her what she really needed. She'd start with redoing the past year. That would put her back on track. She'd go back to nursing school. She'd ignore Lincoln's advances. She'd make better choices.

She would remember the person she'd been raised to be. She'd done her best to run from the gilded cage she'd been in all her life. She'd thought that cage confining. Now she realized it had been safe.

But there were no do-overs in life, only opportunities to move forward. "There's nothing."

"Lunch?" Oregon offered with a sweet smile and shrug of slim shoulders. "A hug?"

She almost cried. It made her realize how alone she'd felt for the past few months. She'd climbed inside herself, hiding the secret of Lincoln's abuse from people who could have helped. She'd lost pieces of herself one bruise at a time. She would put herself back together. For her baby. And for herself.

She moved her hand to her belly.

Oregon moved to the sofa. A slim arm slipped around Grace, pulling her close to the other woman's side. "It'll get better. I know people love to use the phrase, 'I've been there.' But I really have. I had Duke's child twelve years ago. I was younger than you and very alone."

Grace's throat tightened with emotion and tears stung her eyes.

Oregon gave her another quick hug. "It gets easier. And harder. Better. And worse."

Grace laughed through her tears at that bit of honesty. "Thanks. I think."

"I won't lie. It won't be the easiest thing you've ever

done. But you'll have friends. If you stay here, I'll help you any way that I can."

Grace tried to find words to respond to this unexpected offer of friendship. She drew in a breath, felt a little stronger. "Thank you. I know I can do this. The past few months have been rough. But it has to get easier."

"Of course it will. Now let's have a sandwich and then I'll show you my store." Oregon stood and held out a hand to pull Grace to her feet. "If we're lucky we'll get a little peace and quiet before one of the Martin men comes storming in to…"

As if on cue the outside door opened. Brody stepped in, his gaze shooting from Oregon to Grace. "I thought I'd check on you before I head out to the ranch. I've been rounding up a few supplies for Jake."

"I'm good," Grace assured him, standing next to Oregon. "We were just going to get lunch."

"Yeah, you should eat. I don't think you kept any of your breakfast down." His suntanned cheeks turn a little pink. His blue eyes skirted the room, looking at everything but her. "Anyway, if you need anything, Oregon has my number."

"Brody, you don't have to…"

"I know that, Grace. But you came here, and I'm not going to turn my back on you."

"Thanks."

Oregon touched her arm and left them alone.

He glanced away, but not before she saw the hurt in his eyes. She started to take a step toward him but stopped, because it did a cowboy no good to think he was getting sympathy when that was the last thing he wanted. He didn't want her hugs or her apologies. He wanted to get on with his life.

He'd help her. She knew that. But she also knew that Brody wouldn't let her back into his life, not after the way she'd hurt him. That was for the best. She was having a baby. That had to be her focus now.

"Well, I've got to run before Jake comes after me. I doubt I'll be back this evening. If you need anything the store is next door. Put anything you need on my account, and I'll settle up with them at the end of the week. Or you can run over to Duke's."

"Brody, I can take care of myself."

He looked at her, really looked at her, then gave a curt nod. He adjusted that beat-up white cowboy hat he wouldn't replace and reached for the door. "Yeah, I know you can."

With that he walked out the door. Grace was left standing in the center of the small apartment, lost somewhere between needing him to come back and knowing she could do this on her own.

She walked through the door that connected the apartment to the shop and found Oregon arranging paints and brushes on a worktable. Grace entered the room, slightly mesmerized by the merchandise.

"You made all of this?" Grace asked.

Oregon stepped out from behind the worktable. "I did. And you're the reason Brody came home angry, aren't you?"

It wasn't said with malice, just curiosity.

Grace touched a Christmas ornament with a pretty manger scene painted on the front of the glass bulb. "Yes, I'm the reason. I never meant to hurt him. I just wasn't ready and he was so serious."

"People seldom do mean to hurt each other."

At that, Grace touched her bruised cheek. "Oh, some people mean it."

"Yes, some do. But if you weren't ready it would have been wrong to lead him on. That would have been another kind of hurt."

Grace walked away from Oregon and the discomfort of the conversation. She sifted through a rack of handmade skirts, then stopped, her hand hovering as she turned to look at Oregon.

"You're right. It would have been wrong."

So why had she come to Martin's Crossing, to Brody, when she could have gone anywhere? Would she hurt him all over again, being here, needing his help?

Because hurting him was the last thing she wanted to do.

Chapter Three

Brody's knees ached, but it felt good to be in the saddle. The big gelding underneath him moved a bit to the right, ears pricked forward as he watched the cattle they were moving. The day had started out gray and rainy but had cleared, and the air soon turned muggy as the sun heated things up. Their mission was to move close to a hundred head of cattle to a field that hadn't been grazed down.

The beef moved slowly, sometimes stopping to munch at grass, sometimes trying to zigzag away from the herd and take off to greener pastures. Brody kept a steady hand on the reins, trying to keep the gelding he rode from bolting. He could handle riding, but a sudden jerk felt like fire going through his leg. That was what happened when wear and tear dissolved the cartilage in a knee.

After the lunch rush, Duke had left the diner in the capable hands of Ned and joined in to help. As they moved the animals through an open gate, Duke rode up beside Brody.

"You doing okay?" Duke asked in his typical big-brother tone that got under Brody's skin.

"Why wouldn't I be?"

"Could you stop being defensive for one second and just be honest?"

"I'm honest. Why wouldn't I be fine?"

"Well, you've had your leg out of the stirrup more than in. And on top of that, a pregnant woman showed up this morning and it's clear the two of you are more than just friends."

"We're not even friends. And it isn't my baby, if that's what you're thinking."

"No, I wasn't thinking that. What I'm thinking is that you don't like to share anything with your family, and that makes it kind of hard to help you."

"I'm not a little boy. I don't need your help or your advice. If I do, I'll ask."

"Right-o, brother. But you did need a place to put that woman to keep her safe."

"Yeah, I did. And thank you for that. I'm not sure how long she'll stay, but at least she's safe for now."

"Brody, you have to let go of the past."

"I didn't know I was hanging on to it."

Duke rode up to the gate and swung it closed, leaning from his horse to wrap the chain around the post. Brody rubbed his knee, moving it from the stirrup and then putting his foot back in before Duke could catch him. A shot of fear tugged at him, because he knew what arthritis and joint damage could mean for a guy who made his living on the back of a horse. He already knew what it meant to a bull-riding career. He knew what it meant when, late at night, he could barely stand up and walk from one room to another.

The gate secure, Duke turned back to Brody. "You might pretend nothing bothers you, but you're so uptight I'm surprised you don't crack when you walk."

"Oh, you'd be surprised."

Duke's attention shot to the knee Brody rubbed without thinking. "Not too surprised. Can they do surgery?"

"I've had surgery. Last year before I came home."

"Then, why is it still bothering you?"

"I'm actually working on finding out. So if that's all you want to know, let's get back to the barn and treat that other bunch for pinkeye before it spreads."

They rode in blessed silence for a few minutes. Brody started to mention a horse he'd like to look at, but thought if he said anything Duke would feel the need to talk more about the past, about Grace or about his health. Sometimes they forgot he was almost twenty-seven. He had a double degree in special education and counseling. He'd been on the dean's list every year. Stupid, he was not.

"Would it help you to find Sylvia?"

At the mention of their mother's name, Brody pulled back on the reins, surprising the gelding, who sidestepped a few times and shook his head to protest the rough treatment. Brody whispered an apology to the animal and brushed a hand down the horse's dark neck.

"Why bring her up now?"

Duke shrugged and kept riding. "Because everything comes back to her. She abandoned you."

"She abandoned *us*." He didn't like to talk about it. The only person who knew his feelings about Sylvia was Grace. He'd told Grace all about how his world had fallen apart as a little kid. Now, as an adult, he realized it had never been too secure of a world to start with. Sylvia had always been a mess. Their dad had been pretty okay until she'd left.

"That doesn't mean you don't want to find her."

"Why is it that *I'm* the one who wants to find her? Aren't you the least bit curious? Wouldn't Jake or Samantha like to know where she is and what's happened to her?"

Duke directed his horse toward the pen where they'd managed to confine the young steers with the pinkeye outbreak. "Yeah, I guess we all go through periods when we wonder. But I've hired a PI."

Brody caught up with his brother. "You did what?"

"I hired a private investigator. I think it's time to close this chapter. Maybe finish the book and start a new one."

"Poetic. But save it. I'm not interested."

"Aren't you?" Duke swung a leg over the saddle and slid the ground. He looked up at Brody. "I think it would do you a world of good to confront the lady."

Brody didn't know what to think exactly. "I think that I'm fine."

"Yeah, I know." Duke led his horse by the reins into the barn.

Brody took a little longer to dismount. He swung his leg over the horse's rump and was careful to land on his right leg and not his left. It still took him a minute to cowboy up and not cry like a girl. He closed his eyes and took a deep breath.

"Next time we take four wheelers," Duke said from behind him.

Brody opened his eyes to find his brother watching him. "Yeah, good idea. But I do miss being in the saddle."

"So now that we've talked about your knee and our mother, let's forge ahead and discuss the lovely Grace Thomas, barrel racing diva."

Brody shook his head and walked past his brother, leading his horse. "No, I think not."

"You might have to. I just saw a truck pull up out front and I'm pretty sure it's Lincoln Carter."

Brody almost swore. Almost. He tossed the reins of his horse to his brother and hurried through the barn. When he walked out the front door, Lincoln had already gotten out of his truck.

"Where is she?" Lincoln thundered, his face mottled from anger.

"She?"

"You know who I'm talking about. Where's Grace?"

Brody shrugged. "Not a clue. Remember, she left me for you."

"Is that how we're going to play this?" Lincoln asked. "Do I have to put a fist to your face?"

Brody almost said something about Lincoln making a habit of that lately. He bit back the words, which would have given too much away. "No, I guess not. But you know what they're saying about head trauma and moods. Seriously, you should get that checked. You've had more concussions than the average man."

Brody hadn't realized until then that he meant what he said. Not only was Lincoln a bull rider, he'd played high school and college football and taken some serious blows to the head. The giant shift in Lincoln's personality suddenly made sense.

"There's nothing wrong with me." Lincoln insisted. "I just need to find Grace."

"Maybe she doesn't want to be found, Lincoln."

"That's too bad, because I'm going to find her." Lincoln took a step toward him.

"Head on down the road, man. She isn't on this ranch, and if she needs you, she'll call."

Lincoln looked around, then he shook his head. "I'm going to find her."

"I'm sure you are." Brody shoved his hands into his pockets. "Well, I have some cattle to treat, so I'll say goodbye."

"I miss you, Brody."

"I miss you, too, Lincoln. But you're going to have to get in your truck and head on down the road. I'd appreciate it if you didn't come back."

Lincoln pulled off his hat, ran a shaking hand through his hair, then smashed the hat back down on his head. "It isn't my fault she left you."

"I'm not having this conversation. She made her choice about us. And now it looks as if she's made a choice about the two of you. I'd let it go if I were you."

Lincoln made a move; his fist came back. Brody had figured he'd do something stupid, so he moved, letting Lincoln find nothing but air. Brody shook his head and turned to walk away. Lincoln came at him again, a booted foot to the back. Brody fell forward, catching himself against the barn wall and then turning, because a man didn't take a hit to the back and walk away.

"You're a coward, Lincoln," Brody called out, knowing it would work.

Lincoln came at him again. Brody grabbed Lincoln

by the arm. Lincoln pulled back his fist and Brody caught his hand in his own.

"I'm not going to hit you, Lincoln. It would be too easy, and you're the only one around here who likes an easy target. I suggest you leave town before I have you picked up. I suggest you leave the state. That would be the best thing you could do."

"I can't leave."

"You don't have a choice. You either leave, or I escort you off the property."

"Her running to you doesn't mean she's ready to wear your ring."

"Since she isn't here, it doesn't matter."

Lincoln shook free. "I'm leaving."

Brody took a few deep breaths as he watched Lincoln take off in his truck, gravel flying.

"You think he'll find her?" Duke stood behind him, holding the reins of both horses.

Brody reached for this horse. "I doubt it."

"Aren't you worried?" Duke headed for the barn with his big gray gelding.

"She's fine." He busied himself unsaddling the horse, aware that Duke watched him with that steady gaze that saw too much.

"Go check on her. I'll finish up here."

Brody faced his brother. "I'm taking care of my horse."

"Right, but you're tied up in knots worrying about her. You don't have to get hooked up with her again, but you care. Nothing wrong with that."

"I'll check on her when we're finished."

"At least call and warn her that Lincoln is in town,"

Duke suggested as he unsaddled his horse. "You don't want something to happen to her."

Brody's hand went to the chain that hung from his neck. Beneath his T-shirt he felt the ring still in place next to the cross. He'd kept it since the night when he'd planned to propose to Grace. Before he'd had a chance to ask, she'd ended their relationship, telling him they were getting too serious and she wasn't ready for that. He'd kept the ring.

It was a reminder—one he wouldn't soon forget.

Clouds rolled on the southern horizon and the breeze had picked up. Grace stopped on the sidewalk in front of Oregon's, unsure of which way she wanted to walk. She didn't have a plan. She just knew she needed some fresh air. The wooden sign hanging from the overhang of the shop next door caught her attention. Mueller's Christmas Shop. Grace told her about it earlier, about Lefty and his carved nativities and candlelit Christmas carousels.

She walked down the sidewalk to the store and reached for the doorknob. It was locked. That didn't surprise her. Oregon had closed a short time ago. All of the shops in Martin's Crossing probably closed early. Except Duke's No Bar and Grill. It was still open.

Suddenly her phone rang. She reached into her pocket and answered the call from Brody.

"Are you at Oregon's?" Brody asked.

"No, just window-shopping at Lefty's."

"Lincoln was here. I don't think he'll come to town looking for you, but you should be careful. Maybe stay inside."

"Okay, but I'm fine."

"I know you're fine. Just be careful."

As she hung up she heard a truck on the road. It probably wasn't Lincoln, she consoled herself. He wasn't going to risk showing up here when there could be witnesses. The coward in him only struck when no one could see. But she wouldn't take a chance. She was too far from Oregon's, so she went around the side of Lefty's store.

As she ran along the back of the shop, a door opened. An older man stepped out. He waved her forward. "Come inside."

"I'm sorry?" She hesitated and he reached for her arm. Grace froze, unsure. Her heart raced and fear kept her feet planted.

"Brody called me because he knew I'd be here and he wanted you safe. Come inside."

She slipped through the door and it closed firmly behind her. Her legs shook as she stood there in the small living room, unsure of what to do next.

"I'm Lefty Mueller."

"I'm Grace," she said, flicking a quick look at the door, and taking a deep breath. "Grace Thomas."

"It's a pleasure to meet you. Though not under these circumstances," he winked as he said it.

She looked around the tiny living room with the Victorian furniture and heavy wood cabinets built into the walls. "Is Lefty your given name?"

At that the dapper man with thinning gray hair and a twinkle in his gray eyes smiled. "My given name is Matthias, but I'm left-handed. My father always wondered if I would be able to carve, being left-handed." Lefty had moved to a small stove in the kitchen alcove of the apartment. He poured tea from a kettle and held out a cup. "Peppermint tea. Please, have a seat."

She carried her cup to the sofa and sat. Mr. Mueller poured himself a cup of tea and sat across from her in a wing chair that seemed too large for his slight frame.

Humor teased away her nervousness as she considered her situation. She felt somewhat like Alice falling down the rabbit hole. Her entire world had changed— the people in it, her surroundings… Nothing felt familiar or safe anymore. Yet here she sat drinking peppermint tea with a wood-carver named Lefty, who spoke with a slight accent that said he'd been exposed to another language for a large part of his life.

"Would you like to see my shop?" he asked after they'd finished their tea.

"I'd love to." Grace stood, feeling a little shaky as she followed him through the double doors and into his showroom.

As she stood in awe at the many hand-carved nativities and Christmas carousels, he lit candles in an extravagant, triple-tiered carousel in the center of the room. The windmill of the carousel heated and started to turn. The carousel with the nativity figurines began to spin.

"It's lovely. I've seen them before but never like this."

"Thank you, my dear. I enjoy making them. It makes me feel as if I celebrate our savior's birth all year long. Some people light a carousel once a year and enjoy the nativity for one month. I enjoy them daily."

It was obvious he loved his art, his job. The love he felt for it was in each piece he carved. Before she left Martin's Crossing, she told him, she'd buy one to take home.

"You're leaving?"

"I'm not sure," she answered. She hadn't really planned how long she would stay or where she'd go next.

"You have time to make plans. Don't rush yourself." He snuffed out the candles on the carousel and the figurines stopped spinning.

Before they left the store he picked up one of the carousels and held it out to her. "This one is for you. I'll box it up tomorrow and bring it to you at Oregon's."

"I can buy it."

"Nonsense. It's my gift for you."

She gave him a quick hug. "Thank you."

A sudden pounding interrupted the peace and quiet inside the shop. Grace glanced around the room, her heart racing as she searched for a hiding place.

"You're safe." He pointed to the stool behind the counter. "Sit. I'll check, but my guess is that it's Brody Martin pounding my door down."

He left her alone in the shop, her gaze shifting from the back door to the front door. She calculated how long it would take her to reach the back door and run to Duke's No Bar and Grill.

The door between the shop and the apartment opened. She collapsed back on the stool, her legs suddenly weak. Brody pulled off his hat and ran a hand through his dark hair. His gaze took in the room and then settled back on her.

"I would have been here sooner but Lincoln stopped me on the steps of Duke's, and I had to linger over an iced tea."

"He's gone?"

Brody nodded, but his attention fell on Lefty Mueller. "Thank you for taking her in."

Lefty winked at her. "I'm glad you called me, Brody. We had a nice visit over a cup of tea."

"I've had a cup or two of that tea myself, Lefty. I'm sure she enjoyed hanging out with you." Brody settled his hat back on his head. "I'll walk you back to Oregon's."

"I can walk myself, Brody."

"I know you can, but that doesn't mean I'm going to let you."

The two of them stood there facing one another. Grace didn't want this animosity between them. She'd come to him for help. It had been her choice. It had actually been her first thought, to go to Brody.

Lefty took the tea cup from her hand and she gave him a quick hug. "Thank you for taking me in and for the tea. I enjoyed seeing your shop and talking to you."

"You're very welcome, my dear. If you ever need anything, my door is open." Mr. Mueller smiled at Brody. "And you, young man, take good care of her."

"I'm not sure if she wants that, Lefty, but I'll do my best."

Brody took her by the arm and led her out the back door of the shop, over to the back door of Oregon's All Things. She unlocked the door with the key Oregon had given her and stepped inside. Brody took off his hat and followed her across the threshold.

It suddenly dawned on her, what Lefty had said. She grinned as she looked at the big cowboy, hat in hand. "You drink peppermint tea with Lefty?"

He shot her a look that was none too pleased but cute, nonetheless. "Men can drink peppermint tea."

"Of course they can." She sat down on the over-stuffed couch and pulled a pillow to her lap. "Have you eaten? I can make you a sandwich."

"I thought I'd head over to Duke's. What about you?"

"I had a sandwich earlier."

He frowned at that. "That isn't much of a meal. Why don't you go to Duke's with me."

She sat there, the pillow on her lap, and Brody standing tall and awkward in the center of the small apartment. Finally she nodded, pushing aside fear and misgivings to accept the peace offering he'd extended.

"I think that would be good."

She followed him out the door. They walked side by side down the sidewalk and across the street to Duke's. They didn't touch, not even by accident. They didn't speak, not even to comment on the weather.

Peace was a fragile thing, she realized.

When they got to the diner, Brody went up the steps slowly, flinching each time he raised his leg to the next step. She wanted to help. But how did she do that without tackling his cowboy pride?

"Have you considered using the ramp?" she suggested, knowing immediately it had been the wrong thing to say.

Brody shot her a look. "I'm perfectly capable of using steps."

"I know you are, but if it causes more wear and tear…"

He kept going, ignoring her.

When he got to the door he held it open for her. "After you."

She stepped into Duke's. The restaurant was long

and low ceilinged with barn wood-paneled walls and a tin ceiling. The tables were rough wood. The booths along two walls were wood with rustic fabric-covered seats.

A woman came bustling out of the kitchen. She was nearly as tall as Brody. Her auburn hair, shot through with gray, was pulled back in a tight ponytail. She grinned big as she scooted past them with a tray of food.

"Sit anywhere, kids, and I'll be back to take your order in a few."

"Will do, Ned." Brody led Grace to a table where a half dozen people sat together. There was an older couple that smiled as they continued to bicker over something, a couple of men drinking coffee and a younger couple with a little boy.

"Mind if we join you all?" Brody asked as he reached for a chair.

"Sure thing," one of the older men said. "Have a seat, and introduce us to your friend, Brody."

"Grace Thomas." Brody pulled out a chair for her and took the seat next to it. "This is Ian Fisher and his brother, Bill. That's their sister, Ava, and her husband, Chuck, and these are the Lansings." He nodded toward the young family. "Sara and Carl and their son, Clay."

She smiled and thanked them for letting her join them. They all laughed and made jokes about Brody not giving anyone a chance to say no.

He reddened at the joke and looked as though he might wish he'd taken a seat elsewhere. But this was Martin's Crossing, and she imagined if they'd sat alone the rumors would have been rampant. Not that there wouldn't be rumors anyway.

Ned headed their way after refilling coffee for a few diners.

She placed glasses of water in front of them and then pulled up a chair and sat down. "I'm about worn out."

"Long day, Ned?" Brody asked as he picked up the glass of water.

"Long day, long week and longer year. Do you all know what you want to eat?"

"I'll take the special." Brody handed her back the menu.

"I'll take the same." Grace smiled and handed the waitress the menu.

"You got it, kids. Do you want something to drink other than water?" She held up the coffeepot she carried. "Or I can get you tea."

They both declined and Ned pushed herself to her feet and headed for the kitchen. As she walked away, a slim, dark-haired girl came out of the kitchen, a big grin on her face. Grace knew immediately who the child had to be.

"Lilly, what are you up to today?" Brody asked, confirming her suspicions. She watched him change as the girl headed their way. His eyes lit up. He looked amused and protective all at once. The corner of his mouth tilted and revealed the dimple in his cheek.

"I have a horse to pay off, remember?" She sat down next to Grace and studied her long and hard. "So you're the trouble…"

"Lilly." Brody cut her off as he chuckled. "This is Grace."

Grace held out her hand. "Better known as trouble."

Lilly smirked. "Mom said you're staying in the apartment."

"Yes, I am."

Lilly leaned back in her chair and Brody reached over, putting the chair back on four legs. "Down, killer."

"I have to get back to work. Mom and Dad will be here soon." She stood, her attention focused on Grace. "I'm sorry I didn't meet you earlier. I came here right after school."

"I'm sure we'll have a chance to get to know each other," Grace offered.

"Great," Brody murmured. "Maybe we should get our food to go."

"Why would we do that? This looks as if it might be entertaining," Grace teased. It was easy to do when she knew how much Brody liked his privacy.

"We should leave before the whole family shows up," he said, leaning in close. "You're laughing at me now, Gracie, but you wait till you're face-to-face with Jake, Duke and their women. And then there's this bunch."

He inclined his head, taking in the group at the table.

"I do like to see you squirm."

He leaned back in his chair. "They'll eat you alive."

As if on cue, one of the older men turned his attention on Brody and Grace. He grinned as he settled his fishing hat on his head, the stiff bill shading his face but not hiding the teasing glint in his dark eyes.

"Brody, I'm just a wondering when you're going to hang up your running shoes."

"Running isn't good for your knees, Brody." Grace

understood the double meaning but she jumped in anyway. Anything to see his face turn red.

"I haven't been running, Grace."

The other gentleman laughed at that. "Brody, as far as I can tell, you've been running for a year. Looks to me as if it finally caught up with you."

Brody shot her an I-told-you-so look. She'd jumped in, thinking Brody would be the target. But it was suddenly clear that in Martin's Crossing, no one got a break. For the next hour she took her share of teasing. When Brody's brothers and their wives showed up, they made sure Brody took his fair share of ribbing. It felt good to be a part of that crowd, and to spend time laughing and not worrying.

When Brody walked her back to the apartment an hour later, Grace was exhausted but still amused. She'd learned a lot about Brody Martin in their time with his family and with old-timers who'd known him all his life.

"You really rode a bull through the school?" she asked as she unlocked the door.

Brody lifted one shoulder in a casual shrug and reached to push the door open. He flipped on the lights inside and stepped back for her to enter.

"A friend dared me."

"Do you always take dares?" For reasons unknown even to her, Grace's voice softened. She looked up and saw Brody watching her, his blue eyes intent.

She wanted to touch him. She wanted to brush her hands over the dark shadows on his cheeks. She wanted to lean in and inhale his scent.

Instead, she took a step back, knowing that they didn't have a future. She'd broken his heart once.

And Brody didn't trust easily. She had a baby to think about. This was definitely not the time for distractions.

"Brody, thank you. For letting me stay here and for not being angry."

"Oh, I'm still angry, Grace. That doesn't mean I don't care." He kissed her cheek and walked away.

She drew in a deep breath as she locked the door behind him, then leaned against it. A tear slid down her cheek.

She brushed it away because crying did no good. She'd gotten herself into this mess and she'd survive. Somehow.

Chapter Four

Brody sat in the exam room long after the doctor had handed him a sheet of instructions and left. The diagnosis hadn't been a surprise, but he'd been given a royally good chewing out for putting off this visit for so long. He guessed he'd just hoped it would go away. He'd guessed wrong. Rheumatoid arthritis didn't go away. Neither would the cartilage damage in his knee. But at least surgery could clean that up. The upside, if there was one, is that it would probably respond to treatment and even go into remission. Men, he'd learned, had less severe cases of RA than women.

At least he knew the prognosis.

He couldn't sit in this room for the rest of the day, avoiding his life. He pulled on his boots, shoved his hat down on his head and left the exam room behind.

He headed for the waiting room and Grace. He'd stopped at Duke's for coffee that morning and she'd been there. When she'd found out he was heading to Austin, she'd asked for a ride. Of course he hadn't been able to tell her no.

He was going to have to practice if she planned

on staying in Martin's Crossing any length of time. He mumbled, "No, Grace," to himself, then shook his head. He was really losing it.

"No, Grace, I don't need someone to hold my hand," he grumbled. "No, Grace. I don't think I'll give you a second chance," he whispered to himself.

"Are you talking to me?"

She was heading toward him, coming out a door near the exit. *No, Grace.* The words evaporated as she stepped close, a sweet expression on her face, lingering dark brown eyes. She could turn a man into a fool with that look.

"Nope," he said. He'd been talking to himself. It made him half-mad that he couldn't hold on to his anger when she was around.

His gaze went to the baby bump her loose shirt didn't hide. Her hand moved to that bump and her smile faltered. He hadn't meant for that to happen.

"You okay?" Her voice was soft in the quiet room, where a dozen people waited.

"I guess so." He hooked his arm through hers and they headed for the elevator.

"You're lying," she said when the elevator doors slid closed.

"Yeah, I guess."

"Are you going to tell me what's going on?"

He shook his head and pushed the lobby button. "Nope. Where do you need to go?"

"Brody, we're at a rheumatologist."

Yeah, he knew she would put two and two together. That didn't mean he was ready to talk about it.

"Yeah, I guess we are. Where do you need to go?"

Silence for a blessed moment.

"A department store, please. I need a few things that I can't get in Martin's Crossing."

For some reason that lightened his mood. He doubted she'd planned it that way, but he'd take any rope he could grab hold of.

"What? There are things you can't get in Martin's Crossing?" He smiled as he teased her. "I thought the feed store had everything."

"If everything includes grain, rubber boots, lead ropes and work jeans."

"Sounds like everything a person needs."

"Yes, everything a person needs. But what I need the most is my friend," she said, her amusement fading.

"Don't."

He led her across the parking lot to his truck. When he reached to open the door for her, she placed a hand on his arm. He drew in a deep breath and looked down at her. She had a serious look on her face, the kind that went right through him.

"I know you don't want to talk, but if you change your mind, I'm here."

"I appreciate that."

She bit down on her bottom lip as she studied him. "Brody, I do care. We…"

"Don't. We're not a 'we' anymore. Whatever you do or I do, there's no 'we' involved."

"I know that. I'm just saying, I know you're in a lot of pain. And I know your surgery last year didn't go well. There was a lot of damage that they probably couldn't…"

He cut her off, motioning her to get in the truck. "I don't want to talk about it."

"Gotcha. But you know as well as I do that you're going to have to face it."

"It isn't fatal, Grace."

"No, but I'm sure it's life changing."

"Yeah, well, there's been a lot of those moments in the past year." With that, he closed the truck door.

When they got to the mall, he dropped her at the door, then parked the truck. She waited for him at the entrance. Her hand touched his, but then she must have thought better of it because she walked a little ahead of him. He followed her inside.

The first thing she did was head for the baby stuff. He felt a little itchy when she started touching pretty little dresses and pink shoes. He hadn't thought about it, really. That baby bump was going to be a little person in a matter of months. It would wear lacy dresses. Or maybe it would wear jeans and cowboy boots. He picked up a pair of miniature cowboy boots and grinned.

"It's going to be a girl." She stepped next to him, taking the boots from his hand and putting them back on the shelf.

"It's a boy," he teased. "I've heard that boys are always right out front and girls spread themselves around their momma's entire middle.

She looked down, her eyes widening as she covered the bump with her hand. "Do you think?"

He shrugged. "It's what I've heard, but I don't really know."

What he did know was that this baby wasn't his. She wasn't his. He walked away from miniature boots, tiny Wrangler jeans and T-shirts with cute sayings about tough guys and daddies. He didn't belong there.

What was he doing with Grace? She was a Fort Worth princess who was waiting for a prince to sweep her away to his castle. He lived in a single-wide trailer, owned some cattle and had a degree that made him feel smart but would never pay much.

She followed him as he made his way from baby clothing, through women's clothes, and finally to an exit that led to the rest of the mall. He found a bench and sat down. Grace sat down next to him. He glanced sideways at the woman with her softly rounded form in a loose cotton candy pink T-shirt, jeans and boots.

"You go ahead and shop. I'll wait here for you."

"Do you want me to go?" she asked, her voice soft, unsure.

Go? He knew she meant permanently, out of his life. What did he want her to do? "You mean, go get your shopping done? Yes, I'd like that. I'm not really up to walking the entire mall. But I can wait here. I've heard that's what men do. 'Waiting on a Woman.' It's one of my favorite pastimes and a decent country song."

"Brody, I meant I can go home."

"Yeah, I know what you meant. I don't know what you want me to say."

She sighed. "I don't, either. I'm not sure what my next move should be. I can't stay here forever. I know that. But I can't go back to Aunt Jacki's, and I don't want to face people in Fort Worth. I'd like my own space, a place I choose."

"I get that. I guess you're going to have to remember who you are. And remember that we all mess up."

She leaned into his shoulder. "But that doesn't mean there aren't expectations for Howard Thomas's granddaughter. My grandfather has built one of the largest churches in the state. He's respected and known across the country. I don't want to hurt him. Or hurt my parents."

"There are expectations for all of us. Ask Jake and Duke. As Martins, people expect something of us. We founded a town and we're leaders in our community, not that there's much to Martin's Crossing. But the expectations are there. And we're all human."

He was angry, defeated, half in love and still jealous. He leaned back and pulled off his hat. When he did, a timid hand brushed through his hair, smoothing it back. He nearly closed his eyes at the touch. Not a second too late he remembered why he needed big thick walls between himself and the woman beside him. She was all sweetness and soft touches, but she didn't know what she wanted. Scratch that. She knew one thing; she didn't want him.

"Grace, don't," he muttered and her hand dropped.

"I'm sorry. Brody, I'm so sorry for hurting you."

"You've said that before and I get it. But I'm not going back. You can sow whatever wild oats you need to sow, but leave me out of it."

Because that was all he'd been to her. For him, it had been much more. She'd filled in the missing pieces that had kept him strung out and wild for most of his life. He'd started to believe she'd be his life forever, that she wouldn't walk away. No other woman had ever made him believe he could have it.

"I'm going to finish my shopping. But I want you to know I'm sorry. I can't undo what I did last year." She touched her belly. "I can't undo this. I also can't give this baby up. She's mine and I won't let her down, even though I seem to be letting everyone else down these days."

"That's the most important thing, Grace. Be there for him, and if you do that, you've done everything right."

"She," Grace said as she walked away. "My baby is a girl."

"Nope, that's a boy you're carrying, Grace Thomas. I'll eat my hat if it isn't," he called out after her.

The thinnest laugh carried back to him as she walked into the department store. He watched her go, thinking back to when he'd first met her. She'd been traveling with her aunt Jacki, who trained barrel horses. Grace Thomas, socialite, nursing student and granddaughter of a man who pastored one of the biggest churches in Fort Worth, Texas. She'd had it all, but she had wanted to spend a year being a cowgirl on a ranch in the heart of Texas.

He'd loved her fearlessness. And then he'd just plain loved her.

He still loved her, but he was determined not to let it show.

Grace piled everything on the counter at the register. Socks, T-shirts and a tiny sleeper in pale green. It was soft and made her think she could do this. She could hold a little baby in that sleeper and be a mom.

The cashier smiled at her as she lifted the sleeper. "This is sweet. When are you due?"

Grace blinked back tears. "February."

In a matter of months everything would change. Again. She would be someone's mother. She managed a smile for the cashier, who continued a steady stream of conversation about babies, clothes and the weather. Grace tried to keep up but her thoughts were trailing far behind, still caught up in the thought of being a mom.

The cashier looked up, her eyes locking on someone just beyond Grace's left shoulder. Grace knew from the appreciative look on the other woman's face that it was Brody. She glanced over her shoulder and saw that she'd been right. She also saw the slightest grimace on his face just before he winked, pretending everything was fine.

She wasn't fooled. Not by a long shot.

"Ready to go?" he asked.

"Yes. I just have to pay."

The cashier watched them, and Grace knew the other woman thought they were a couple, parents-to-be. At any moment she would say something, maybe congratulate them.

Brody picked up her bags as she paid. Just when Grace thought they would escape, the cashier called out, "Best wishes to you both with that new little one."

Grinning, Brody turned back to the lady, a big grin on his face. "Thank you, ma'am. We're both real excited."

As they headed toward the exit Grace glared at him.

"What?" His eyes widened and he stopped walking. "Did I do something?"

"You're terrible." But she didn't feel even the slightest bit of irritation.

Instead, she laughed.

Brody chuckled, the sound rumbling over her.

"Were you going to break her heart?" he asked. "She was all excited for us."

"I know. It's just I'm not sure what to say to people."

"Thank them and move on. You're having a baby. People are going to comment."

"Yes, I guess they will. The hardest thing is…" She shrugged and couldn't admit it to him.

He opened the truck door for her to get in, and as she got settled, he opened the back door of the extended cab Ford. As she buckled up, he leaned in the open door. His hands were now free of her purchases. He must have put them in the backseat.

"The hardest part is what?" he pushed.

She avoided looking at him.

"Grace?"

"I'd like to go to church. But…"

"But you're afraid of what people will say?"

"Yes, and how they'll look at me."

He stood there for a minute looking at her, and her heart stumbled over his nearness. His spicy scent wrapped her up, and slowly her hand stole to his face. His eyes closed, then opened. He shook her hand off his cheek and backed away.

"Probably best not to do that," he said as he put a few feet between them. "You were telling me about church?"

"I want to go to church. I *need* to go to church."

He sighed. "I'll take you Sunday. It'll be easier to walk in with someone."

The offer unsettled her, but she knew it would be easier to walk in with him. The next time she could do it on her own.

"Thank you."

The door closed softly. For a moment she was alone in the quiet of the truck.

"It's all about you now, sweet girl," she told the baby bump beneath her hand.

Brody got in and started the truck. His quick glance landed on her belly. "You okay?"

"I'm good. She's starting to move. It's only a flutter, like butterfly wings brushing my abdomen, but it makes it all very real."

He reached into the backseat and tossed her the bag he'd carried out of the store. "I bought these for him."

Him. She shook her head and laughed a little. When she opened the bag she wasn't surprised to find a tiny pair of cowboy boots.

"She'll look cute in these."

He shook his head. "He. I kinda like the name Lyle."

She didn't know what to say, and he was looking at her so intently, so seriously, she couldn't laugh.

"Lyle? For a girl?"

"For a boy. After Lyle Lovett. You know he's from Texas, right?"

"So is George Strait."

"I guess you got me there. You could name him George." He grinned as he eased into city traffic. "So have you called your folks?"

"I've talked to them, I just…" She glanced out the window at city traffic and the Austin skyline. "They're going to be disappointed."

"Maybe, but they won't be devastated. Your parents are good people."

"Yes, they are. But they wanted so much for me."

They drove in silence for a few minutes.

"You keep talking in past tense. You know your life isn't over, right?" Brody reached to turn down the radio. "You're having a baby. People do it every day. They still have careers. They still get married and have good lives."

"I know. It's just that…" She brushed a hand across her cheeks. "I used to sit on the bed with my mom and we'd talk about what I wanted for my life. We talked about weddings, about being a nurse, about the home I'd have someday."

"You can still have those things."

"What about Lincoln?"

He gave her a quick look. "Do you still want Lincoln?"

The question made her head feel fuzzy. Did he think she wanted to spend her life with a man who had beaten her? A man who didn't want the baby she carried? As the thoughts spun through her mind she realized that Brody didn't have to think highly of her. She hadn't given him reason.

She'd shattered him when she'd broken up with him. She hadn't expected that to happen. For some reason she had thought Brody, like her, wasn't interested in settling down just yet. He was chasing a world title. She wanted a year of just being young and chasing her own dreams. "No, Brody, I'm not interested in Lincoln. I just need to figure out how to keep him from hurting us."

"I think you'll have to get a restraining order. Tomorrow you can talk to Jake's lawyer."

Of course the Martins had connections. They were ranchers, but they were businessmen, too.

"Okay. Brody. Thank you for everything. I'll make it up to you."

"I don't need you to make it up to me, Grace. You knew when you decided to come to Martin's Crossing that I wouldn't turn you away. I'll do everything I can to help you, but I don't need you to make anything up to me. What's done is done."

Yes, what was done was done. Her aunt Jacki had encouraged her to find herself, to experience life before settling down. Now Grace wanted a do-over.

The thought of a do-over was disconcerting with Brody Martin sitting next to her. He was her past. She doubted he would be her future.

Chapter Five

Brody woke up early Saturday morning, way earlier than he'd planned. He put on a pot of coffee, swallowed a couple of pills and then headed to the barn, moving slow but better than when he'd first woken up. The walk did him good, getting the kinks out and loosening up his joints.

The last person he expected to see at the barn this early was Duke. He assumed his older brother would be having breakfast with his wife-to-be and their daughter. Or he'd be at the restaurant serving the breakfast crowd. Instead, Duke was tossing bales of hay on the back of the truck.

"What are you doing up and around so early?" Duke asked as he tossed another bale on the growing pile.

"It isn't that early. Sun's up."

"Yeah, guess it is." Duke pulled off his work gloves and tossed them through the open window of his truck. "I'm taking these over to Jake's place. Want to ride along?"

"Doesn't Jake have his own hay?"

"Yeah, he does. But Breezy talked him into getting

a couple of llamas. I don't know why, but he agreed to it."

"It's because he's going to be a daddy, and he wants to give Breezy anything that makes her happy," Brody answered. Instantly his thoughts turned to Grace, because she was alone, with no husband to make her happy, make her feel safe and cared for.

She was strong, but it wouldn't be easy.

"Climb in. We'll head that way," Duke said as he headed for the front of the truck.

Brody didn't remember agreeing to go, but he climbed in anyway, grabbing the handle on the side of the door frame to pull himself into the cab of the truck. Duke shook his head, but didn't comment.

As the truck headed down the drive, in the direction of Jake's place, Duke cleared his throat. "Heard any more from Lincoln?"

"Nope. But I think she needs a restraining order against him."

"Probably," Duke agreed. He shot Brody a quick look, his gaze landing on Brody's hands. "What did the doctor say?"

"Not much."

Duke let it go. He pulled the truck up to the barn near Jake's place. "There's an extra pair of gloves in the toolbox if you want to help unload."

It felt like a test, and Brody never liked to fail a test. He grabbed the gloves when Duke opened the metal box in the truck bed. Duke grabbed his own pair and slipped them on, pretending not to watch Brody pull the gloves on his swollen hands. Two could play the game of pretending not to notice.

"What is Breezy going to do with llamas?" Brody

asked as he reached for the first bale of hay, careful to school his features as he wrapped his fingers around the wire that held the bale together.

"Nothing." Jake's voice came from behind him. "Absolutely nothing. But she's always wanted one, and how could I say no?"

Brody lifted the bale of hay out of the truck and carried it to the barn. "You've never had a problem with the word in the past."

"Yeah, well, things change. Women do that to us."

Brody changed the subject. "How are Rosie and Violet? Do they know they're going to have a little brother or sister?"

Rosie and Violet were the twin nieces that Jake and Breezy were raising as their own since Jake's twin sister, Elizabeth, and Breezy's brother, Lawton, died in a plane crash. The twins had brought the couple together.

"They're good, and we haven't told them yet. They're only three. I doubt they're going to understand too much. If you're coming to church tomorrow, you'll see them then. Why don't you come over for lunch after?"

"Yeah, I'll be there." He grabbed another bale of hay, wiggling his fingers around the baling wire, taking a deep breath and lifting. "Heard from Sam lately?"

That was his trick: steer the conversation to something other than himself. It was good to ask about their little sister. She always had something going on that they could discuss. He glanced at Jake before heading to the barn with the hay.

"Yeah, she's planning on graduating next summer. She's excited about working close to home."

"Good for her. I've missed her."

Brody said nothing else, because he didn't need to repeat that he thought his brothers had made a mistake when they'd sent Sam away to boarding school and then college. All to keep her away from a guy they thought would get their little sister in trouble. "We've all missed her. Holidays are never really enough," Jake said as he grabbed the bale of hay Brody reached for.

Brody pushed him away. "I can unload hay."

"Of course you can. Why all the small talk, brother?"

"It's just talk, Jake. We humans do that. We communicate to learn information."

"Right. Of course we do." Jake backed off and let him take the bale. "But you're especially chatty this morning."

"Just being a good brother." Brody stepped past Duke and tossed the last bale on the pile.

Jake followed him into the barn. "Do you want to move into Lawton and Elizabeth's place? Breezy mentioned it the other day. It's sitting there empty, and she's worried it'll get vandalized."

"I have a place."

"I know you do. But it isn't big and it isn't…"

"It's fine." He pulled off the gloves. "I'll see you at church tomorrow. I've got work to get done at my place."

"Not so quick," Jake said as he put a hand out to stop him from walking away.

Brody shook his head. He should have stayed in bed. "What?"

Duke walked into the barn holding a manila envelope in his hand. He wasn't smiling. "We have something to discuss."

"Great." Brody sat down on a bale of hay. "I really don't want to talk. The two of you are going to have to realize I'm not a kid. Worry about your women, your children and your businesses, and let me worry about my life, my health and my future."

Jake sat down next to him. The sun was streaming in through the open barn door and a momma cat joined them, stretching out in a sunny spot on the floor to watch birds in the rafters. Brody pulled off his gloves and waited.

"We're family, Brody," Jake started with what Brody thought was the obvious. "We raised each other. We survived together. That isn't something we can undo just to make you more comfortable with your need for privacy."

"Right, I get that. But for now give me space."

Duke tossed the manila envelope at him. Brody caught it.

"Open it," Duke ordered.

Brody hesitated, then lifted the flap and pulled out the papers. He read over the information. Looked at the pictures attached. And then he shoved it all back inside the envelope.

"Well, I guess that's good to know," he said, smiling at both brothers.

Duke leaned against the wall. "You wanted to know, and I thought it was time."

"Right, okay. Thanks. I think I'll walk back to my place. I'm going to work on that fence today so it'll hold horses come spring."

Jake stood when Brody stood. "I can give you a ride."

"I can walk. I learned how about twenty-six years ago. I don't want to talk. I don't want explanations. I'll see you at church tomorrow."

They let him walk away.

The problem was that he didn't really want to. He wanted to ask questions. He wanted to know how they felt about the information in that manila envelope. Since he'd taken the first step, though, he kept going.

He went home and built the fence. And he considered how it would feel to give riding lessons to foster children in the area. He'd learned at an early age that horses could keep a kid grounded, keep them focused on something other than pain and anger. He wanted to do that for children who might not have the opportunity otherwise.

The last thing he wanted to think about was that manila envelope on the counter in his trailer. He kept working, stretching barbed wire from post to post, one strand at a time. The work kept him focused. The pain in his hands took his mind off all the questions he'd like to ask but might never get answers to.

By late afternoon he was worn out. He barely made it up the front steps of the trailer, ready for a glass of tea and a sandwich. As he headed for the fridge, he ignored the envelope. He wouldn't look at it again. He wouldn't think about that day when Sylvia Martin had headed down the drive in her old Buick. His brothers had held him as he'd cried and fought them, wanting to go after her.

Their dad had been at a livestock auction somewhere and hadn't known until he'd returned home late that night. By then she'd been long gone.

Brody took out the bread and tossed two slices on a plate. The only thing in his fridge that didn't smell sour was a package of bologna. He had some not-too-stale chips to go with it and a few pickles.

The phone he'd tossed on the counter buzzed and vibrated across the avocado-green Formica. He took a sip of sweet tea and glanced at the contact name. Grace. He tried to continue making his sandwich, but he couldn't ignore the call. What if Lincoln had found her?

He answered.

"Brody, I have a roast. I mean, I know you probably don't want to join me, but I thought…"

He sighed, waiting for her to finish. While he waited, he fought off the urge to tell her about his day, about the envelope.

"Brody?"

He blinked back to awareness. "I'm here."

"I shouldn't have called."

"I don't mind that you called."

"You have a right to keep your distance. I know we can't go back to the way things were. But I've been sitting here alone all day and I'm tired of talking to myself."

He grinned. "So you're saying talking to me is better than talking to yourself."

"Something like that. I just need a friend."

Yeah, he could admit it, he could use a friend tonight, too. "I'll be there as soon as I get cleaned up."

Thirty minutes later he parked in front of Oregon's All Things. He thought about going back home. He could tell her he just wasn't up to it tonight. Needing Grace brought back too many memories, some of them good, most of them he didn't want to revisit. He definitely didn't want to say goodbye again. And he figured that was where they were heading as soon as she figured out her next move.

The second he reached to restart his truck, her door opened and she stepped outside. He watched as she swept a hand through her short blond hair, and then that same hand went to her belly. She saw him watching and he imagined she hesitated. Seconds later she headed for his truck, barefoot. She loved to go barefoot.

Grace opened the passenger door of the truck and leaned in. "Were you thinking about leaving?"

He pulled the keys out of the ignition. "It might have crossed my mind."

"I make a really great roast. Come in. It doesn't have to be complicated. And I owe you. A lot more than dinner."

"I'm coming, Grace."

As easy as that, he climbed from the frying pan right into the fire.

Grace reached for his hand as they walked. He looked as if he needed a friend. But he'd always had that look about him. Even when he played the part of the love-'em-and-leave-'em cowboy that most people thought him to be.

She'd learned from Aunt Jacki that he avoided serious relationships. When she'd met him she'd made it her mission to find out why. What she'd discovered was a man who knew how to be a friend. He knew how to listen. But he didn't give easily of himself.

The relationship that had developed between them had frightened her. She hadn't been looking for anything serious.

When they entered her apartment she made a beeline to the coffeepot and poured him a cup. It gave her a minute to collect herself. When she turned he was standing at the window looking out, his back straight, stiff. She set the coffee down on the tiny table and rested her hand on his back. She felt him sigh, then relax beneath her touch.

He turned to face her and she saw that he'd pulled on a plaid shirt over a T-shirt and hadn't bothered to button it.

Not thinking, she reached to button it for him. He shook his head and pushed her hands away.

"Grace, don't."

"Let me help you," she whispered, leaning in close. Her hands hovered near the top button. "We all need help sometimes. I came to you because I knew you would keep me safe. You're here, and I don't think it's because you wanted roast."

"Probably not."

She took that as a yes and started with the top button, working her way down. When she finished she reached for his hands. His fingers were red and swollen. She lifted them, rubbed gently.

"When did this happen?"

He shrugged. "It started a few days ago but today is the worst. Building the fence probably didn't help."

"No, it probably didn't. Sit down and tell me what's

going on. And don't tell me it's nothing. It would do me good to hear someone else's problems."

"That would help you out, huh?" He grinned and the light filtered back into his blue eyes. She loved that sparkle of humor.

"Yeah," she teased. "It would."

He sat down on the sofa, and she sat across from him on the chair.

"Where should I start? My hands? Or maybe with the fact that Duke found our mother."

Grace sat in stunned silence, unable to say anything. She knew what this meant to him, what his mother's disappearance had done to his life.

As she tried to come up with the right words, she saw his hand settle on his knee, rubbing absently. She got up, needing some way to help him. She'd noticed a heating pad in the cabinet. She found it and took it back to his chair, plugging it in and setting the temperature before settling it on his leg.

"What's that for?"

"It will help. And you also need to use ice to help fight the swelling and inflammation."

He closed his eyes and leaned back. "I thought it was just from bull riding."

"What did the doctor tell you?"

"Rheumatoid arthritis. And my knees are paying the price because of bull riding. I guess when it started I just thought it was from the rough treatment over the years and the surgery not going well."

"No, I'm sure you didn't consider it. Did the doctor give you a prescription?"

"Yeah, and a couple of shots. But could we not talk about the RA? It is what it is and I'll live with it."

"Okay, so about your mom?" She sat down next to him, but not close enough to touch.

"You're not giving me a break today, are you?" He opened his eyes and grinned at her. She got a little lost in the blue of his eyes.

"Not a chance."

"She's in Dallas in a nursing home. She has dementia."

"I'm sorry."

"I'm not sure if I am. I mean, I don't really know her. She left years ago. She walked out on us and now what? I'm supposed to feel bad for her?"

"I know you, Brody. You might growl a lot, but you have a big heart."

"I feel a lot of things when I think of her, but nothing that makes sense," he admitted, his voice going soft.

"Maybe if you go see her it'll help?" she suggested.

"Yeah, I've said for years that I want to find her. Now I'm not so sure I want to face her, though."

"I don't blame you."

They sat in silence for several minutes, then she stood. "Let's eat. Maybe after a somewhat decent meal you'll be able to think clearly."

"Can I help you do anything?"

She kissed his cheek. "I can do it. You rest."

She left him alone on the couch. Taking the roast out of the slow cooker, she placed it on a plate with potatoes and carrots that were soft from cooking in the juices of the meat. She'd bought rolls, and she heated them in the oven as she made gravy.

"It's ready," she announced as she carried a platter to the table.

She stilled, setting the plates on the table as quietly as possible. Brody was asleep on her couch, his legs stretched out and his arm under his head. She reached for the blanket on the arm of the nearby chair and covered him. He didn't move.

She sat down in the chair and watched him sleep. Of course he would need rest. That was a symptom of RA. She was sure he knew that. He studied everything. Back when he rode bulls he used to study videos of rides that went wrong and the ones that went right. He would watch them over and over, analyzing what caused a fall and what moves meant staying on. He'd take notes, then he would talk about it until she cried uncle.

Suddenly, her cell phone rang. She glanced at it and her heart hesitated just a beat when she saw her mom's number pop up. They hadn't talked in a couple of weeks. Unfortunately, now seemed like the worst time to have a conversation with her parents.

"Mom..." Before she could say anything else, she started to cry.

"Grace, honey, are you okay?" Hearing her mom's concerned voice on the other end, thousands of miles away, only made it worse. The tears streamed down her cheeks and the hand she swiped across her eyes did nothing to stem the salty wetness that trickled free.

"Mom..." She started again and then sobbed. "Oh, Mom, I'm so sorry for messing everything up. I should have stayed in school."

"Grace, is everything okay?" her mom asked. "Of course everything isn't okay. What's wrong?"

Grace left the living room and walked out the door to stand in the yard, surrounded by the quiet of Saturday evening in Martin's Crossing. In the distance she heard cattle.

"Mom, I'm pregnant."

"Grace, oh, sweetheart."

"I'm pregnant and—" she had to say it "—Mom, Lincoln has been abusing me."

There was a sharp pause. "Where are you now? Is Jacki there?"

"No, she's in Florida. I'm in Martin's Crossing. I just didn't know where else to go." Grace moved across the small grassy area at the back of the building.

"You can go home. You know that. Your grandparents are scheduled to fly out in a couple of weeks. They were going to make a few side trips, but they'll come home sooner for you."

"I don't want to do that to them. I just need a little time to get myself together."

"In Martin's Crossing?"

"I'm staying in an apartment on Main Street. There are people here to help me."

"We can come home. We can leave this week," her mom said in a rush.

"No, don't do that. Dad has dreamed of this trip for years. I don't want to be the reason he calls it off."

"You're more important than this mission."

Grace closed her eyes. "I know you feel that way, but I'm okay, and I don't want you to have to come home because of me. I'm a grown woman and I can do this."

A hand settled on her shoulder. She turned around and saw Brody. He winked, and she believed what she'd told her mom. She could do this. She wasn't alone.

Brody was inching his way back into her heart again. Or maybe he'd never left. But she couldn't go there. Especially not now.

"If you need us, call. You have family," her mom repeated what Grace already knew, but hearing the words felt good.

"If I need you, I'll call." Grace leaned into the arm that had circled her, pulling her close. "You and Dad are okay?"

"Of course we are. But I need to know that you're okay, that you're safe."

"I'm safe. Don't worry, I'll go back to school and I'll get back on track."

"Of course I'm going to worry."

At that Grace smiled. "I know you'll worry, but it's going to be okay. I'm going to make sure I'm safe and then I'll go home. I can probably sign up for the spring semester."

"You'll get through this, Grace. And we'll be home soon to help you."

They said goodbye, then Grace reached for Brody's hand. He led her back into the house and she let him, because it felt good to have someone take charge.

"You should have woken me up," he said as he let go of her and poured himself a fresh cup of coffee.

"You obviously needed the sleep."

He lifted the cup to his lips but grinned over the rim. "Can't stop being the nurse, can you?"

She shook her head. "No, I guess it's what we do in my family."

"That's not a bad thing, you know."

"No, it isn't, is it?"

"Oh, good, make this about me," he grumbled good-naturedly.

"I'm happier making it about you. I think you need to be reminded that your brothers and Sam have always been there for you. You have a tendency to push people away."

"Yeah, well, I need to figure this out on my own."

"You haven't told Duke and Jake?"

"I'm sure they've figured it out but they're giving me space. You know—" the corner of his mouth lifted "—when you stomp around, quiet and unapproachable, people tend to give you space."

"I've noticed that. I'm not sure why you do that."

"Less complicated. People don't get in my business, ask how I'm doing or expect too much."

"Until me?" she asked, as she sat down across from him.

"Yeah, you're kind of a thorn in my side," he teased.

"I'll go with you, to see your mother. If you want."

"No, I don't think so. When I'm ready I can do this on my own."

"Wouldn't it be easier with a friend?" She studied his face, the firm set of his mouth, the blue eyes that caught and held hers.

"I'm not sure anything can make this easier, Grace." He pushed back his chair and stood. "Do you want water? And to stop talking about this before we ruin a good meal?"

She followed him to the sink. It was a mistake. She knew before she got up and took those few steps. But she couldn't stop herself. When he turned around, she was there, waiting for him.

She touched his face, tracing that serious expression with a fingertip and stopping on his cheek where a dimple hid, waiting for his smile. But he didn't. Instead, his breath held, and she reacted in kind. He leaned close enough that she thought she felt his lips brush hers, but there was still air between them as he held there, just a breath away. The moment stretched between them, connecting them.

Brody suddenly stepped back, shaking his head. "This is wrong. I'm all about helping you out. I'm even okay with dinner. But I don't think either of us needs this complication right now."

Of course they didn't. Grace put distance between them, trying to get her emotions firmly in check. Neither of them needed more regrets.

The small flutter in her abdomen caught her by surprise. *No, baby girl*, she thought. *I don't regret you.* She only regretted that she hadn't waited for the right man. She hadn't waited for the person she would spend her life with. She hadn't waited for a man worthy of her, worthy of her child.

She knew one worthy man, and his name was Brody Martin.

Chapter Six

The blow-dryer almost kept Grace from hearing the pounding on the front door Sunday morning. She heard a few short raps, then a pause and a few more raps. She shut off the blow-dryer and glanced out the window. Brody stood on the stoop, freshly shaved, his hair still damp, his plaid shirt unbuttoned over a T-shirt.

She went to the door, opening it to let in cool morning air and the spicy scent of his cologne. She tried to pretend it didn't matter. After their dinner last night she should take a step back, let things cool off. Instead, she stood in the doorway reliving their almost kiss.

"How are you this morning?" she asked as she motioned him inside. "I have coffee for you. I only drink one cup so there's almost a full pot."

"Thanks." He made his way to the kitchenette and poured himself a cup. "Go ahead and finish getting ready. We have time."

"I'm almost done." She stood in front of him, unsure. She really disliked being unsure. "Want me to button your shirt?"

"I'm fine." He sat down at the table, sipped his coffee. When she continued to look at him, he cocked an eyebrow at her. "What?"

"I don't mind."

He leaned back in the chair. "I'm fully capable of buttoning my own shirt. This is just easier, and I choose easy over a daily struggle. I can button my own buttons. I can even cook a decent dinner, fix a fence and saddle my own horse."

"I know you can, I just…" For some crazy reason she started to cry.

So this was what it meant to be an emotional, pregnant female. She swiped the tears away and tried to get mad at him, but she couldn't. He muttered something under his breath, shoved back his chair and he was at her side, gathering her in his arms.

His lips grazed the top of her head. "Shh, I'm sorry. I'm taking steroids and you're hormonal. Probably a bad combination."

She nodded against his shoulder and his arm circled her, keeping her close.

"Go get ready. And I'll have a cup of coffee that isn't cold," he whispered, his breath warm on her ear.

It was good advice. She would finish getting ready and she'd manage to get control of her heart, her emotions. She had a little person who needed her to focus on the future. To do that she couldn't become distracted.

It would be easier if Brody was a stranger to her, and not the man whose secrets she knew and kept. Because there was a side of Brody that no one understood. Yes, he was charming. He played the part of the wild cowboy. But he was the furthest thing from that person he portrayed himself to be.

Deep down, Brody Martin was good, with faith and convictions that kept him grounded, and able to step away from entanglements that would cause him to stumble and forget himself and his faith.

When she came out of her room ready for church, Brody was sleeping on the couch. For the second time in two days. She sat on the coffee table and reached for his hand, but she stopped herself. Instead, she sat there, torn between waking him for church and letting him sleep.

His eyes opened and he blinked a few times, clearing the hazy, sleepy look. "I fell asleep."

"Yes, you did."

He sat up, sighing. "I didn't sleep much last night."

Neither had she, but probably for different reasons. "We should go. It's almost ten o'clock."

"If you want we can leave my truck and walk down the street to church."

"That would be good. I could use some fresh air."

They headed down the sidewalk in the direction of the church that sat on several acres at the end of Main Street. The morning was warm and the sun was bright. Maybe walking hadn't been such a great idea. The heat made her a little nauseated, and her steps slowed as they walked the short distance to the Martin's Crossing Community Church.

"Are you okay?"

"A little sick, but it'll pass."

Taking her hand, Brody led her across the street to a small green area with a fountain and a few benches. "Let's take a break."

"I don't want to be late for church."

"If we're late, we're late. If you pass out, we won't make it at all."

"Passing out isn't on my to-do list." She sat on the bench and he sat next to her.

"When was your last doctor's appointment?" he asked.

"I've only had one appointment. I need to find a doctor. I just thought I would wait until I got home to Forth Worth."

"Maybe you shouldn't wait."

She shrugged off the suggestions. "I'm not having any problems. I just had a little nausea and lightheadedness from the heat."

"I'm not an expert here, Grace, but I think the standard thing is a monthly visit to the doctor, right?"

"Yes," she admitted.

"If you need me to go with you, I can. If you don't want me to go, I'm sure Oregon would."

The church bells began to ring and Grace watched as latecomers ran up the steps and into the church. It was a pretty building, classic in design with a vestibule at the front, a tall steeple with a bell tower and stained glass windows. She didn't compare it to her grandfather's church, all glass and stone, and covering several city blocks.

Brody stood, his hand absently going to the chain on his neck before reaching for her hand. She smiled at the habit of reaching for the cross on that chain. She took his hand and stood, carefully, waiting to see if the sickness had passed. It had, and she prayed it wouldn't return.

They approached the pretty little building that had been the center of the community since the beginning of the town's history. It had been added on to over the years, she'd learned from Lefty Mueller, but the stained glass windows, the bell tower and the wood-work were original.

When they entered the church the congregation was standing for the opening hymn. Brody led her to a pew where Jake sat with his wife, Breezy, and Duke, Oregon and their daughter, Lilly. The two of them squeezed in next to Lilly.

People stared. She'd known they would. But they weren't cataloguing her sins. She knew that, even as heat rushed to her face. They were watching because they knew Brody and she was at his side. They were speculating on what their relationship might be.

She could tell them they were friends, barely. She'd broken his heart, but he was good and kind and still willing to help her.

The sermon that day was on peace. The music seemed to coincide. But for Grace the day was about being in God's presence. About making things right and about finding a way back, because she'd spent more than a year running from her life.

The closing prayer ended the service, but Grace took a moment longer, her head bowed. A hand touched hers. She looked up at Brody, who was stand-ing next to her.

"You okay?"

"I'm good," she assured him. "Thank you for bring-ing me."

He shrugged. "Anytime. Jake said to invite you over for lunch. Breezy has something for the grill and Duke is bringing the sides."

Lunch with the Martins. She settled her gaze on

Brody for a heart-stopping moment because he was looking down at her with the softest look in his eyes. He had only fastened a few buttons of his shirt, and he was standing there as if this didn't matter.

But it did. To her it mattered. It mattered because she needed his forgiveness. In her quest to live she'd overlooked the feelings of this man. She'd overlooked her faith. She hadn't really thought about the consequences.

While she was in Martin's Crossing she would make things right with him. She would help him face his past. And his future. She owed him that much.

"I'd love to have lunch with your family."

Brody told Grace to wait at the church. He'd get his truck and pick her up so she didn't have to walk. She'd argued that walking was good for her. He'd argued back that he wouldn't have her passing out on him.

It was also a chance for him to get a few minutes to himself to think, because she was getting under his skin. Or maybe she'd been under his skin from the moment they'd met.

Some people, he'd heard, learned from their mistakes. He didn't seem to be one of them. But he was fighting the part of himself that gave in too easily. It was that same part that had wanted to find Sylvia Martin, not to tell her how angry and hurt he was, but to know her. She had a story. She had a reason for leaving. He wanted her story.

He knew Grace's story. She'd been loved, sheltered, and great things were expected from her. But she'd needed out of that ivory tower to find herself. She hadn't been looking for love, just for adventure.

She definitely hadn't wanted a broken-down cowboy for that future. She'd also made it pretty clear that she planned on going home to Fort Worth. It would serve him well to keep that in mind. Somehow he had to shed this need he had to take care of her, to keep her close.

Big words for the guy pulling up to the church and getting out to open the door for that same woman. She smiled up at him, all sunshine and sweetness, her blond hair framing her face, her dark brown eyes intent on his.

He closed the door as she buckled herself in, thanking the good Lord that every now and then he was in full control of his common sense.

As they drove out to the ranch he kept conversation to a minimum. It was easier that way, to play country music on the radio, pretending that every Keith Urban song wasn't about falling in love. Why was it that when a man fell in love, he suddenly had to sing dozens of songs about the subject?

He reached to turn down the radio. She stopped him.

"I like that song." She pushed his hand away from the button.

"Great." He brushed a hand through his hair and focused on the road.

"Someone told me about your plan to buy horses and start a riding program for foster children," she said.

"Someone did, did they?"

"Yes, is it true?"

He looked heavenward before answering, "Yep."

"It's a great idea."

"I thought so."

He had other good ideas. One dangerous one included pulling to the side of the road and kissing her. Another better idea had him heading the truck for Fort Worth and taking her home to her family. Instead, he turned at the entrance to the Circle M, driving under the arched, wrought iron sign.

"I'm trying to have a conversation, Brody. Maybe we can talk about something other than pregnancy and Lincoln."

"And arthritis?"

"Yes." She studied his face as she responded. "I'm interested in what you're planning."

He didn't doubt that. "Can I turn the radio down now?"

In answer she pushed the power button.

"I want to use my degree and I think this is a way to stay on the ranch and still help kids. I remember what it was like, growing up a little bit lost and disconnected. If it hadn't been for my horses, I might have had a different story."

"So you'll give kids a chance to spend time on the ranch?"

"That's my plan. I want them to learn about horses, how to care for them and how to ride them. But it's more than about riding. It's about giving them a connection with animals. Because sometimes when we feel no one else is listening…"

He pulled in the drive of Jake's house and parked behind Duke's truck. "I know it sounds crazy."

"No, it sounds amazing, like something you would think of."

He felt his neck flush. "Yeah, well, I'm a sensitive kind of guy."

He hopped out of the truck, escaping her praise. That moment with her meant more to him than it should. When he opened her door she didn't get out.

"You are a sensitive kind of guy," she finally said. "And what you're doing is great. So when someone tells you that, say thank you."

"Okay, thank you." He reached for her hand to help her out.

Lilly met them on the front porch of the house. She was sitting in a rocker with the twins, her grin wide. Brody gave her a long look, enough of a warning that she glanced away.

"What took you so long?" she asked, rocking back and forth with a couple of sleepy little girls.

"Are you in charge of my time card?" Brody asked, wiping his boots on the door mat.

"Nope, just wondering. I am in charge of…"

Brody pushed the door open. "Go on in, Grace."

Grace looked from Brody to Lilly. "I think I'd rather hear what your niece has to say."

"I'm in charge of ma…"

"Go." Brody pushed her gently through the door. She winked at Lilly as she went inside.

Brody closed the door behind her, then pinned his niece with a look she wouldn't misinterpret. "Don't."

"But you taught me the art."

"I helped you out with your parents, but I don't need help."

She had the nerve to laugh. "Oh, I think you do. I'm very good at this, and you do not have game."

"No, I don't." As the words slipped out he groaned,

and of course she laughed even harder, bringing the twins to life. Rosie and Violet giggled, even though they didn't know what they were giggling about.

"At least you're honest." She quieted the twins, who were still smiling big, watching him. "Let me know if you decide to take me up on my offer. And by the way, Dad accidentally got your mail. He wonders why you're seeing a rooma…rooma-something."

Rheumatologist. He didn't explain to his niece; instead, he thanked her for the help and went inside.

Grace stood in the center of the massive living room with tile floors, a stone fireplace and leather furniture that would take up his entire trailer. He thought about Lawson and Elizabeth's house, empty since Breezy had married Jake. He couldn't quite bring himself to consider his sister and brother-in-law's home for himself. It was big, too big for a bachelor.

It had a lot of memories. And he couldn't go there today, couldn't think about the sister he'd lost and her husband.

"It's a pretty place," Grace said as she stepped to his side. "I waited for you. How did the inquisition turn out?"

"Did you think you'd have to rescue me?"

She smirked. "Maybe. I heard you made wedding invitations for Duke and Oregon long before he proposed. If their daughter gives you a hard time, you deserve it."

"Yeah, I probably do. I didn't go easy on Duke and Oregon. But this is different. They have a…" He didn't finish the sentence. "I'm sorry."

Her hand rested on his arm. "Not your fault. I teased and I shouldn't have. I…I've missed you."

That statement was best left alone. He looked toward the door and found it easy to disengage. "We should see how things are going in there."

At that moment the door opened and Lilly bounded in, a twin on each hip. "You'll hurt your back," he warned.

She shifted the girls a little higher. "I'm young, not old and gimpy."

He laughed. "You're cheeky."

"That, too." Off she went toward the kitchen, the twins laughing as she broke into a gallop, whinnying for effect.

"That kid is great," Grace observed.

"Yeah, she really is."

Together they headed for the kitchen. Even before they got there he could hear Duke giving Breezy a hard time about something she'd put on the meat. And Oregon was laughing about the new recipe he'd tried for the slaw. Family small talk. He remembered back when they were kids, the laughter, the teasing and family dinners were in short supply. Jake said he stayed far from the kitchen these days because he'd spent too many years trying to feed four kids with ramen noodles and mac and cheese. The kitchen was his least favorite place to be.

"Your family is great," Grace said in a soft voice. "Not that mine isn't. They are. They're just different."

"A little quieter and classier?" Brody mused with a wink.

Her mouth quirked and one shoulder lifted. "Maybe quieter."

A sudden urge to kiss her came over him and he

stepped away, fighting temptation. "I should help out. Have a seat and I'll get you a glass of…milk?"

"I'm not five. A glass of water, please."

"Coming up."

His phone rang. He lifted it from his pocket and frowned at the caller ID. Grace arched a brow. He showed her the name and she shuddered.

But he answered. "Lincoln?"

"Yeah, it's me. Listen, I want to know where Grace is. Her family is worried."

Brody knew better. She'd already talked to her parents and her grandparents. "If they're worried, it's probably because you're calling them."

"I need to see her, Brody. We're having a baby. That means something to a guy."

Brody knew better than that, too. "Yeah, but most men don't hit the woman that's having their child. I think it's better if we end this conversation. I only answered to tell you to leave her alone, Lincoln. She's talked to a lawyer and we're going to get a restraining order."

A sharp laugh sliced through the phone. "We. Are the two of you a 'we' now? I don't think so, Brody. You were her summer romance before she went back to reality. If she's there now, she's just using you all over again."

Brody held the phone close to his ear, but Lincoln was yelling, and from the grimace on her face, he saw that Grace had heard.

"I don't mind, Lincoln. I'm always willing to help out a friend. And if you ever decide to get help, I'll be here for you."

The phone went dead.

"Well, that was fun," Duke said, a firm hand on Brody's shoulder. "You know how to pick your friends."

He shrugged it off because the past was the past. Grace sitting on that bar stool in front of him didn't mean she was his future. Or that he had to make the same mistakes all over again.

The definition of a fool was someone who kept doing the same thing over and over, expecting a different outcome. Brody Martin wasn't anyone's fool.

Chapter Seven

The best thing about Grace's tiny apartment that Sunday afternoon was her sofa. She could have climbed the narrow stairs to the bedroom, but after Brody dropped her off she couldn't imagine making it that far for the nap she'd been craving. Her entire body screamed for rest.

But first she followed Lefty Mueller's advice and made herself a cup of peppermint tea. And with it she ate the zucchini bread Jake and Breezy Martin's housekeeper, Marty, had made before her date with Joe Andrews.

After her snack, she grabbed the blanket off the back of the couch and collapsed. There were moments, such as this one, when she thought she might not return to Fort Worth. She loved this community she'd found and the friends she'd made. She loved everything about Martin's Crossing. Then the image of a cowboy with faded jeans and a bent-up cowboy hat edged into her thoughts.

Brody. She knew better than to dream of him. Once upon a time she'd hurt him. And now she was having his best friend's baby. Her baby. She had to focus on being a good mom. On doing what was best for the child she would have.

She drifted off to sleep, only to be startled awake by a heavy pounding on the front door. She sat up, still half-asleep, and started to yell at Brody that he didn't have to pound the door down. But the pounding went beyond what Brody would ever do.

She stumbled to her feet, reached for her phone, her heart stuttering with fear. She dialed as she ran for the bathroom. As she locked the door, she heard Lincoln yelling that she'd better open up or she'd regret it.

She sank to the floor as Brody answered.

"Lincoln is at the door. Brody, I'm scared." She drew up her knees and leaned forward, the hand that held her phone to her ear trembling. "I can hear him out there. He's going to break the door down."

"Hang on. I'm going to put you on the phone with Breezy. She'll talk to you while I call the police and head that way. Grace…"

She nodded silently, because she couldn't manage to speak.

"Grace, I'm on my way. He won't hurt you again." She whispered, "I know. But please hurry."

Then Breezy was on the phone, telling her everything would be okay. "Grace, Brody and Jake are on their way. They've called the local police. Stay in the bathroom with the door locked. And grab the hair spray if there is any in the cabinet."

Hair spray? She scrambled to her knees and crawled to the cabinet, rummaging through the contents. And then she heard the loud splintering of the front door.

"He's inside." Her voice shook as she told Breezy.

But she had the can of hair spray in her hand. "How did I ever think he was charming? Why did I do this to myself?"

"We all make mistakes, Grace. We don't always see people clearly until we've spent more time with them."

He was pounding on the bathroom door, rattling it on the hinges. "He's here. He's trying to get in the bathroom."

"They're on their way."

Grace scooted into a corner as the door creaked beneath Lincoln's assault on the wooden frame. She raised the hair spray, praying Breezy knew what she was talking about. The door gave a little. And then she heard the sirens.

Lincoln gave the door one last kick, because he wasn't a person who gave up easily. She waited for him to burst into the bathroom. But instead there were voices: a police officer, Jake and Brody.

"Grace, let me in." It was Brody's voice, quieter, more reasonable and soothing.

She got to her feet and hurried to unlock the door. Brody pushed it open, causing it to creak as it scraped the floor. As he stepped into the room she flew into the safety of his arms.

He held her, his arms loose around her but his voice calm, making her feel less shattered, more whole. "He's in police custody, Grace. This time they'll have him on a few charges."

Tears streamed down her cheeks, and her throat tightened with fear, with emotion. "I never thought he'd do this."

"He was my best friend for years and I never would have thought he'd turn into this person. But he's going to jail and you're safe." He looked at her with a lop-sided grin. "What were you going to do with that hair spray?"

She looked at the can she still held. "I have no idea. Breezy told me to find hair spray and I did. Maybe she just wanted to keep me busy?"

He chuckled. "Maybe. I guess you can ask her."

She was stronger than she thought. She was able to smile and laugh. Lincoln hadn't taken everything that made her the person she was. She walked to the front door and watched as the patrol car drove away. She watched Jake and Duke carry tools and wood up the sidewalk to fix the door.

"What do I do now?" she asked, not really expecting him to have the answers.

"I guess that's up to you. Oregon said you can stay at her place."

"That's sweet of her." Grace watched as Duke and Jake worked on the door and the door frame.

Jake stepped back. "We'll do what we can with this tonight, but it looks as if we'll need a new door. We'll get one in the next few days and put this back together if Grace wants to come back."

"I'd like that," she answered, feeling more positive than she would have expected.

Brody adjusted that bent-up cowboy hat, pushing it back just a little. "Then, I'll take you to Oregon's?"

"Yes, let me pack a few things."

When they pulled up in front of Oregon's place, Grace grabbed the small bag she'd packed and got out. Brody walked with her but she redirected him away from the house and toward the barn. He had questions in his eyes that he didn't ask. She kept walking and he remained at her side. Horses grazed in the field. It was early evening and the distant hills were bathed in lavender and gold as the sun set. She breathed in deeply, loving it here.

Maybe it was this place, the land and the people that kept her from moving on. For a few years she'd felt unsettled, as if the carefully constructed pieces of her life weren't fitting together the way she'd planned. Even in Stephenville with her aunt, riding barrel horses, living free of the constraints of her life in Fort Worth, she hadn't felt this way. Here, in Martin's Crossing, she felt as though the missing pieces were coming together.

It was never too late. She knew that. All of her life she'd been taught to believe in second, third and even fourth chances.

"It's a pretty evening," Brody said as they stopped by the fence. A gray gelding headed their way, his ears forward, his soft brown eyes studying their faces and then shifting to the dog that ran up to Brody.

Brody reached to pet the horse, rubbing its jaw and then down its smooth neck. The horse tossed his head, then pushed against Brody's hand.

"It is pretty. I can't imagine going back to Fort Worth."

He didn't look at her. "When do you think that will be?"

"I'm not sure. I know I have to go home, but it isn't easy."

He moved away from the horse and the fence, facing her. "I guess you don't have to leave in a hurry."

"No, I guess I don't. But I can't stay and take advantage of your family's generosity. I'm going to have to make some real plans soon."

He fingered the silver chain that hung around his neck. She knew a cross hung from that chain and that he'd worn it since his sixteenth birthday. He always rubbed that cross before a ride. He didn't believe in lucky charms, he'd once told her, but he did believe in prayer. And he believed what that cross stood for. The words had always been followed with a good-natured wink because he didn't want anyone to see beneath the surface.

She knew what was beneath the surface, though. A man who could be counted on; a man who kept his promises. A year ago he promised her he'd be there if she ever needed him.

But he'd also promised her he wouldn't make the mistake of loving her again.

Brody needed to go. He had work to do. And he needed space from the woman at his side. She had a way of getting in his head, making him think too much. She made him think about himself, about forgiving, about the future.

"I'll walk you back to the house," he offered. He kept his hands shoved in the pockets of his jeans as they walked.

"Thank you for driving me out here today."

The conversation went on that way for the next few minutes. She talked about nothing. He gave answers that meant nothing. When they neared the house, Oregon came out, Lilly at her side.

"We're going to Duke's for dinner," Lilly chimed in before Oregon could say anything. "He said to tell you to come, too."

"I think I'm gonna head home, and I have a feeling Grace will crash early," Brody answered.

"There are leftovers in the fridge, Grace," Oregon offered. "Or I can bring you something from Duke's."

"I'll be okay. You all go ahead and enjoy," Grace assured Oregon with an easy smile.

"You'll be staying in Lilly's room. It has the blue spread and too many horse posters. You can't miss it."

"Thank you."

Oregon and Lilly headed down the road on foot, the dog running alongside them. Mother and daughter held hands as they walked. They were close. And Oregon had done everything for her kid. Brody admired her.

He knew Grace would do the same. She'd put everything into raising her child.

"You'll be a good mom," he said. She didn't need to hear it from him, but the words were as honest as the blue sky stretching over them meeting the horizon, touching the hills.

"I hope so," she said, looking up at him.

"It's a fact." Man, he was losing all sense of balance with her. Those dark brown eyes had a way of undoing his common sense.

"Why are you doing this?"

"Doing what?"

"Making me feel as if what I did, the way I broke things off, was okay, as if I'm not a horrible person."

When she frowned he touched her cheek, then slowly slid his finger to her chin, drawing her face up so that he could lose himself in those eyes all over again. "You are a good person. We all get a little lost sometimes."

Her eyes closed and one tear dripped down her

cheek. He caught it on the end of his thumb. Then he forgot that kissing her was the worst idea ever. He captured her lips, soft and sweet, with his. He heard her soft sigh, felt her melt a little as she relaxed against him. He wrapped an arm around her, holding her as he brushed his lips across hers.

She felt so right in his arms that for a minute, he couldn't believe this was wrong, that it would ever be wrong. Her lips moved to his temple. He captured her mouth again as her hand landed on his chest. Her fingers settled on the chain at his neck.

He tried to shift away but her hand had found what he'd kept so carefully hidden. His broken heart, his broken dreams...

She fumbled to pull the chain out from under his shirt. "Brody, what is this?"

She held the ring, still attached to the chain, dangling next to the cross he always wore. The diamond glistened as she held it up, her eyes seeking his, seeking answers.

He pulled the chain from her fingers. He should have guessed this moment would come someday, the moment when she knew that he had cared far more for her than she'd cared for him. He'd been a friend, a good time. She'd been the woman he'd planned to marry.

"I guess that's an engagement ring," he answered, hoping to sound as though it didn't matter. "Unfortunately I never got the chance to give it to the woman in question."

She closed her eyes, her hand covering her face. "Oh, Brody."

"Don't worry about it. I'm not pining for something or someone."

"Then, why do you keep it?"

He brushed off the question. "I keep it to remind myself that people can't be who we want them to be. It's a mistake I won't make a second time."

Just like the kiss they'd just shared. A warm but distant memory. A mistake.

"I'm sorry," she whispered. "That night?"

"Yeah, the night you broke up with me. I took you to that restaurant thinking I would propose. It's all water under the bridge now. Why don't I walk you in, show you where things are, then I'd best head back to my place."

It should have been easy. He took her in the front door of the house, through the small living room, down the hall to Lilly's room with all the horse posters. He opened the closet and found that Oregon had already cleared space for her.

"Is there anything you need before I go?"

She took hold of his hand as they walked back to the kitchen. "I should have been better to you."

"It's been a year and…" He didn't know what else to say, but he didn't get a chance.

She pulled the chain out of his shirt again. "You've moved on but the ring is still here, reminding you."

Yeah, reminding him that the next time she came around he wouldn't be a fool. He eased away from her.

"Don't worry, though, I'm not planning another proposal." He headed for the back door. The dog was there, waiting to be let in. When he opened the door, the border collie slid past him into the house. "I'll see you."

"Brody, we should talk."

He glanced back over his shoulder. "No, I think all

the talking has been done. Don't worry about it. You have a little guy in there who needs you a lot more than this guy does."

He headed out the door, sorry that he had to walk away but knowing it was the smartest thing he'd done all day. Unfortunately he did look back, and people were right, looking back was never a good idea. She stood at the door watching him leave, the border collie next to her. The ring hung cold against his chest as he climbed behind the wheel of his truck.

Chapter Eight

Ever since Grace had found the ring on Monday, the chain had felt cold and heavy around Brody's neck. It was time to let go of the past. He pulled the silver chain off his neck, then tossed it on the counter of the trailer. The cross and the ring skittered across the countertop. He picked them up and put them in a cup so they wouldn't get lost.

A truck pulled up outside. That would be Jake, wanting him to help load cattle for the livestock auction. Brody grabbed his cup of coffee and headed out the door. His dog followed him down the steps, chasing a barn cat across the yard. The yellow tabby swiped at the dog, sending it yelping back to his side.

"I told you to leave that cat alone. That's a fight you won't ever win." Brody eased down the last step. "Come on, girl. You can come with us, but you've got to stay in the truck."

"Ready to go?" Jake shook his head at the dog. "A Maltese? I can't even imagine what brought you to this point."

"Sally's a good dog."

"Yeah, and she serves a dual purpose. Dog and dust mop."

"Original," Brody muttered. "Did you look over my proposal for making the riding school a nonprofit?"

"Yeah I did, and it looks good. I'm going to look over our books and see how much we can funnel into it."

"I don't think it'll take much to keep it going once we buy the horses and tack. And there's a certain amount that can be written off," Brody offered.

"I told you it's a good plan."

Brody leaned against the truck, his hat pulled low to block the morning sun. He gave Jake a long look. "Then, what's the problem? I can see it in your eyes."

"The problem is that you aren't being honest with any of us about your health, and that concerns me. This is a huge undertaking. There are going to be lots of kids counting on you."

"You think I won't stick with it?"

Jake shook his head. "That isn't what I'm saying. Do you have to turn everything I say into a fight?"

"No, I guess I don't have to."

Jake headed around the front of the truck. "Get in."

Brody climbed in the truck, Sally hopping in after him, then taking a seat between the two men. Jake started the big old dual-wheel diesel that they used for pulling the stock trailer.

The truck eased down the drive, the stock trailer rattling along behind. Jake finally glanced his way. "You got a letter from a rheumatologist. That doesn't surprise me, but it would be nice to know what's going on."

"Really? It sure surprised me."

Jake shifted and eased the truck through an open gate onto a dirt road that led to the field where they would load the cattle they were selling. "I think we all put two and two together. So you've been to the doctor."

"Yeah, I've been to a couple. I have rheumatoid arthritis. It isn't the end of the world, and the medication they've got me on is helping."

"I'm glad to hear that," Jake said as he pulled the truck around and backed the trailer to the gate. "Did they tell you what to expect?"

"Pain, a lifetime of medication and hopefully bouts of remission. It's all good."

"All good?" Jake asked, a brow shooting up as he asked.

"Yeah, all good. I'm not going to let it knock me down, and I'm not going to get so bad that I can't work with these kids. Like you always told me, I just need to put on my big-boy pants…"

"And get over it." Jake finished the sentence. "Brody, I was a kid back then, and I didn't know what to say."

Brody opened the door to get out. "We were all kids doing the best we could. Don't beat yourself up. You got me through the worst of it."

"We got each other through," Jake replied. "About the riding camp, though."

"Jake, I'm going to do it. It isn't something I came up with overnight. It was my plan in college. It was my plan while I was riding bulls. I've got a pretty good bundle of savings. I can buy horses and saddles, and I can keep building my herd. With or without you, I'm doing this."

"I'll do what I can to help." They were walking through the gate when Jake grinned, a sign that the heavy conversation was over. "So what about Grace?"

"Grace is a lesson learned. I got over it. Got over her."

"I can't imagine you wanting to get over her."

"Yeah, well, she isn't interested. The night I was going to propose…"

Jake cut him off with a choked sound. "You proposed?"

"No, I was going to. But before I could she broke it off. Said she wasn't ready for anything serious and she was sorry if she gave me the wrong idea. She just wanted to have fun before she went back to school. And the next week she was dating Lincoln, and I was heading home because I couldn't ride until the surgeon cleared me. Which he never did."

"That's pretty rough."

"No big deal. Let's load these cattle."

They had penned the herd the night before. The Angus moved around the small enclosure. Jake's attention refocused on the cattle.

"Yeah, I guess we'd better get to work. But, Brody, if you need to talk…"

Brody walked off, shaking his head. "Getting married has made you and Duke soft. You want to talk about things now. I can do without that."

Jake laughed. "Yeah, it's a whole new world. But I can tell you, marriage has a lot to recommend it."

"I'll keep that in mind. Now keep your focus on these cattle and we'll get them off to market."

Jake opened the back of the trailer, still laughing. Brody had put up with sullen, moody brothers for most of his life. Now he had to put up with the opposite. He wasn't sure which was worse.

The cattle went in the trailer with few problems. Jake was latching the door when Brody's phone rang. He pulled it out of his pocket and then took a few steps away from Jake, because he didn't need his knowing looks or comments.

"Oregon, what do you need?"

"Brody, I'm leaving for work in a few minutes, but I wanted to see if you could come by and check on Grace. She isn't feeling too great. I told her I think she needs to make a doctor's appointment soon. Morning sickness is normal but she's in her second trimester and it should be…"

"Uh, okay, you can stop with the pregnancy talk. I don't know anything about trimesters or morning sickness."

"No, you don't, but she needs someone."

"I didn't say I wouldn't check on her, just, you know, the pregnancy stuff. It's a little above my pay grade."

Oregon laughed. "Gotcha. No pregnancy talk. But you will check on her."

"I will check on her."

He slid the phone back in his pocket and headed for the truck's cab. Jake joined him, sending him a sly look. "She okay?"

"Far as I know. I'm not the pregnancy expert."

Jake started the truck and pulled out slowly. The cattle weighed down the trailer and made it a little wonky as the animals shifted. "You know, when you took that vow at sixteen, I didn't think you would stick with it."

Another subject he didn't want to talk about—that vow he'd taken during a youth service at church. "Well, I have. It's not a big deal."

"It's pretty commendable."

"This is why I keep things to myself," Brody grumbled. "Because my brothers have turned into women."

Jake laughed, the way Brody had known he would. That was a perfect example of how a woman changed a man. Maybe he should be glad he'd dodged that bullet.

Jake pulled off the dirt trail and onto the driveway. "So I'll drop you at Oregon's?"

"That would be good."

"It's been an enlightening day," Jake said as he pulled down the drive to the stone cottage. "Think about moving into Lawton and Elizabeth's place. It's empty and has a lot fewer stairs."

"I'll keep that in mind, but I kinda like my trailer."

"Lawton's is just as far off the beaten track. Duke and I wouldn't be in your business there anymore than at the trailer."

Brody grinned. "I guess that's true. And it has that handy walk-in shower for a guy with bad knees. See you later."

He jumped out of the truck and headed for the front door of Oregon's place, his dog racing ahead of him. Oregon's car was gone. When he opened the door he saw Grace curled up in the big, overstuffed chair, an afghan covering her still form.

"Bad morning?" he asked as he sat on the arm of the chair.

"She didn't have to call you. I'm fine."

"Of course you are. You're pale." He put his hand

on her forehead. "And clammy. Symptoms that definitely point to a person who is fine."

"I can't argue with you right now."

"Another sign of illness—a woman who can't argue."

He slid down next to her in the giant chair and pulled her onto his lap. Sally, not taking the hint, jumped up in the middle of them, licking Grace's face, then curling in a ball on her lap.

"You smell like cattle." She leaned into his neck. "I like it."

"That's really strange, you know." He tucked her head under his chin and inhaled. "You smell like spring."

He should stop, because this wouldn't end well. He knew the signs just as well as he knew signs of illness.

"Today you make a doctor's appointment. If you don't do it, I'll do it for you."

"I'll call."

"I'll go with you," he whispered into her hair, into the scent of springtime and jasmine. "You don't have to do this alone."

It was a mistake. A big mistake.

But before he could dwell on it, she was off his lap and running down the hall.

Brody's words were so sweet, so sincere. Grace wanted to stay in his arms, in the comfort of his embrace. But that was wrong for many reasons. Unfortunately, or maybe fortunately, a wave of nausea rolled through her stomach. Brody's hand held her arm and she twisted, trying to move away. He let go and she hurried down the hall to the bathroom.

She didn't get sick. The nausea passed but her skin was cold and clammy, her eyes unfocused. Water ran in the sink and Brody moved around the room. He placed a cool, damp cloth in her hand and she settled it on her eyes for a minute, taking deep breaths and letting her stomach settle.

"Come on, I'll help you up."

She didn't look at him, but he took her hand, hauling her gently to her feet. He let go of a ragged sigh and pulled her close, holding her against his shoulder as she breathed and the world righted itself.

"You have to go to the doctor."

"Oregon gave me the number," she told him as they walked back down the hall.

"Have a seat and I'll get you a glass of water. I'm sure you need to stay hydrated."

"Water is pretty hard to keep down." She sank into the chair and reached for the afghan. "Brody, you don't have to do this."

"Do what?" he said as he walked away.

"Take care of me." She didn't want him to feel responsible for her. She could see the pain in his eyes. She'd betrayed him. She'd showed up on his doorstep carrying his best friend's baby.

"Right," he called out from the kitchen.

A few minutes later he returned, a cup in his hand.

"Drink this." He placed the cup in her hands.

"Brody, I don't want you to think you have to stay here all day. I know you have things to do."

"Can we just forgo the arguments for now, Grace?" He sat down on the edge of the nearby couch. "You're here. I'm here…"

"Thank you," she whispered, closing her eyes against another wave of nausea.

"Drink your tea," he ordered.

She held the cup up to her nose, inhaling the scent of ginger. She looked up at him, questioning what definitely wasn't a glass of water.

"It's ginger tea. I found it in the cabinet and I've heard it's good for morning sickness."

"This is just something you know off the top of your head?" She sipped the tea. It was peppery but good.

"A friend in college said it worked for her."

She sipped more of the tea and felt better as the tea settled her stomach. Unfortunately the nausea ended with sudden cramps. Brody took the cup from her and set it on the table as she pulled her legs up, closing her eyes as the pain held on.

"That's it. We're going to the hospital. Right now."

"I don't need the ER. I'm sure it's nothing."

"I'm not willing to take that chance. Wait here while I go get my truck. I'll be back in five minutes."

She nodded. What else could she do? As much as she wanted to spare Brody, she knew he was right. She needed help today. She needed to see a doctor. And she needed Brody.

Grace somehow dozed in the emergency room, even on the rock-hard bed with the IV in her arm. Even with the sound of people going back and forth, coming in and out of the cubicle to check on her. She woke up when the door slid open. Brody gave her a cautious look and she motioned him in.

"Have you heard anything?" he asked as he took a seat on a nearby stool.

"I'm dehydrated and slightly anemic. Or I was dehydrated." She pointed to the IV bag. "Now I'd just like to go home."

The word *home* took her by surprise. Especially when the word brought forth images of Martin's Crossing and not Fort Worth.

"But you're okay? The baby is okay?"

"We're both okay. I should have known, though. Shouldn't I have known the symptoms of dehydration?"

He grinned. "Calm down. You've been through a lot, and I doubt you were thinking about the symptoms of dehydration."

She closed her eyes. "I'm hungry."

"Good to hear. You haven't been eating much. As soon as we leave here, I'll get you whatever you want to eat."

"Chocolate cream pie from Duke's."

"Not until you eat your dinner."

She lifted a brow at that. "Wow, you sound like someone's dad."

As the words left her mouth, she immediately regretted them. "I'm sorry."

He didn't say anything. She opened her eyes and reached for his hand.

"It's okay. We men all come programmed with the twenty phrases dads are supposed to say."

A nurse entered the room, smiling first at Brody, of course, and then at Grace. She held out a clipboard with discharge papers. Her gaze slid to Brody as she spoke to Grace. Grace's eyes followed the same path, and she didn't blame the nurse. What woman wouldn't be drawn to a gorgeous cowboy with his handsome face and a smile that melted a woman's resolve to be strong?

"Did you tell Daddy we couldn't tell yet if this is a little boy or girl?" The nurse held out a pen for her to sign the papers.

Grace peeked at Brody, watching as his cheeks turned red beneath his tan. She hid her smile.

"I'm not..." he started.

Grace cut him off. "He's positive it's a boy, and he's already bought cowboy boots."

"Of course he has." The nurse handed her a stack of papers. "Don't forget to make that appointment with Dr. Aarons. And remember, drink more water. Let this handsome cowboy take care of you."

"Of course, thank you." Grace started to sit up. The nurse shook her head.

"I know you're in a hurry, but you have to leave the IV with us." The nurse removed the port and put gauze on Grace's arm, holding it tight. "There you go."

She gave them a final smile before leaving them alone. The mom and the cowboy who wasn't the baby's daddy. Grace slid off the bed, unprepared for the hand that reached to steady her.

"Take it easy. And remember, I was right when I said you had to go to the ER. So let this handsome cowboy take care of you," he joked, stepping a little too close.

She sighed and slipped her feet into the shoes she'd left next to the bed. "Yes, oh, wise one. Now get me a piece of chocolate cream pie."

Last year her heart had broken a little when she'd

ended their relationship. Now, knowing this wasn't real between them, it broke her heart a little bit more.

She couldn't let him take up room in her life that she needed for herself, to be strong, to be a mom. She had to get back on track, back to the plan that had always been there, just put on hold.

As much as her heart wanted him, she couldn't. Not only because of her plans, but because she'd hurt him once. She knew that being here, pregnant, was hurting him all over again.

It didn't matter that he smiled as if this wasn't hurting him. It did hurt. And she knew in his heart it mattered.

A lot.

Chapter Nine

Fall should bring cooler weather, Brody thought as he headed up the sidewalk toward Duke's No Bar and Grill. This close to October there should have been some relief from the summer heat. Today there was none. The temperature was in the nineties and humidity was high. He took off his hat and swept a hand through his hair as he reached the steps.

On second thought, he bypassed the steps and took the ramp that Grace had suggested. Why not save himself the trouble of overworking his knees?

Cool air greeted him inside Duke's. And a crowd. For a Friday afternoon the place was packed. He waved to a few friends and they motioned him over. He headed in their direction.

"You all going to the rodeo this evening?" he asked as he took a seat at the end of their table.

Boone Wilder leaned back in his chair, a toothpick in his mouth. "Yep. You going to be there, old man?"

"Probably."

"We could team rope. Like the old days," Boone offered.

The old days, before Boone had joined the army and gone to Afghanistan. "Think I'll skip it this time."

"Oh, come on." Boone kept it up. "For old times' sake."

"You aren't any better in the saddle than I am."

At that, Boone grinned. "I can still beat you."

"Probably so."

Yeah, everyone had a story. Boone's included a family that nearly had lost their ranch, time spent overseas and a life that needed rebuilding.

Ned headed for their table, a coffeepot in one hand, menus in the other.

"What are you having, Brody?" She pulled up a chair from a nearby table. "And take your time. My feet are killing me. Let me give you some advice. Don't eat the soup. Your brother went crazy with the spices."

"I'm not having the soup," Brody responded as he picked up the menu.

"Ned, are you griping about my soup again?" Duke headed their way, a big grin on his face. "A man tries to experiment and he gets nothing but grief."

Ned laughed at that. "Boss, there are times when a little experimenting in the kitchen is a good thing, and times when it backfires. That soup ought to be poured down the garbage disposal."

"Joe liked it."

She shook her head. "Joe lived in the town manger last year. His sanity is in question."

Duke sat down next to Ned. "Brody, are you going to help me out tonight?"

"Help you with what?"

"We're taking a few steers in for the steer wrestling."

Brody pointed to the chef's salad. "I'll take salad and no soup. Maybe some bread?"

"Got it, baby boy." Ned hauled herself to her feet and rubbed his face. "I thought you'd never have to shave those pretty cheeks, but look at that, stubble."

"I shave." Brody blushed as he brushed her hand away.

"Because you hope it'll make more whiskers grow on that baby face of yours." With that she walked away, still laughing at her own humor. The guys at the table snickered because it had been Ned and she could get away with it.

Brody shook his head and looked at his brother. "I'm starting to agree. You need new help."

"I heard that, Brody," Ned yelled as she went through the door into the kitchen.

"Hearing like an elephant," Duke whispered.

From the kitchen she yelled again, "And I heard that."

Boone leaned close. "I don't think she heard, I think she guessed that you'd say something."

The door to the kitchen opened, and Ned stood there with a piece of pie on a plate. "Boone Wilder, I'm holding your pie hostage."

"I apologize, Ned." Boone grinned big and even winked to soothe things over.

Brody relaxed. Yeah, it was good to have friends. It was good to forget the woman staying at Oregon's, because she kept him tied up in knots.

One of the guys at the table, Eddie Jackson, leaned forward, pushing his drink out of the way. "Brody, is it true you're looking for some good, gentle broke horses?"

"Yeah, maybe a half dozen to start."

"Why don't you use the horses you've got on the Circle M? Surely you have broke horses on that place," Boone said.

"Yeah, we have horses, but I'm looking for something with a little less fire than the horses we raise. Something a kid can ride."

"I have a nice gelding," Eddie said. "It was my kid sister's but she's moved on to boys."

"Let me know if she wants to get rid of it."

"Will do, and we have a few saddles around. They could use some work, but I'd let you have them cheap," Eddie offered.

"What are you going to do with kid-broke horses, Brody?" Foster Douglas asked from the end of the table. "You already planning a pony for that baby of yours?"

Brody's world went dark. He took a breath and heard Duke clear his throat. With more calm than he would have imagined, he reached for the water glass Ned had left for him. "I'm not sure what you're talking about, Foster."

"Isn't that your woman living at Oregon's?"

"No, actually, she's just a friend."

Eddie glared at Foster with a look. "She was dating Lincoln."

Foster had the good sense to look embarrassed. "Sorry, I just thought…"

"No problem."

Brody got up and headed for the cash register. "Hey, Ned, could I get that salad to go?"

"Sure thing, baby boy." She walked through the

double doors from the kitchen. "As a matter of fact, I kinda thought that might be the case."

She set a plastic container on the counter. "Don't let it get under your skin."

"I know." He pulled out a ten and handed it to her. "Keep the change. And promise me someday I'll find a woman just like you."

She winked. "If I was thirty years younger, I'd marry you tomorrow, Brody."

He put a hand to his heart. "I do love you, Ned."

He leaned across the counter and planted a kiss on her cheek. She laughed and shooed him away.

"Go spread that charm elsewhere, Brody. I'm immune to you Martin boys."

He took his dinner and walked out of Duke's. He glanced across the street to Oregon's shop. Grace was with her, helping. The town's fall festival was just around the corner and Oregon had a lot to do in order to have enough inventory.

He just hoped Grace wasn't overdoing it. He should check on her. Then again, he shouldn't. The other day he had told Grace to get plenty of rest. He'd almost asked if she was drinking enough water. Then he'd reminded himself it wasn't really any of his business.

She wasn't his business. She could stay in Martin's Crossing or she could go back to Fort Worth. Either way, she wasn't his. That baby wasn't his.

The past few days he'd done his best to give her space, knowing she was fine. Oregon could take care of her. He needed to get his bearings back.

His dog missed her, though.

He headed for his truck, and Lilly came running

out of the shop and headed his way. "Uncle Brody, wait up."

"What's up, Lil?"

"Mom said to ask if you could give me a ride home. I want to brush Chief and get him ready for tonight."

"You know I can. Is your dad going to make it home in time to get him loaded in the trailer, or do you want me to haul the two of you to town?"

"He should be home in time, but if he doesn't, that would be great."

"Okay. Tell your mom you're going with me."

She hugged him and ran off. "Thanks, Brody."

Lilly had the energy of a Texas tornado. Last year when he'd first come home, she'd made life easier, kept him smiling. He'd do anything for Lilly.

When he pulled the truck up to Oregon's, Lilly didn't come out of the shop alone. She tugged Grace along behind her. Grace, whose belly had rounded a little in the past couple weeks. He wasn't sure if a guy was supposed to notice, but he did. And he felt a strange sense of longing he hadn't expected and didn't want to define.

The truck door opened and Lilly leaned in. "Can Grace have a ride home?"

"Of course." Why not? He enjoyed torturing himself. He moved the file on the seat next to him and shoved it in the pocket of his door.

Grace slid in next to him. She smelled of cinnamon and pumpkin.

"You going to the rodeo tonight?" Small talk, he told himself, would make the ride a lot easier.

"I think so. That's why I'm headed home. I'm going to rest up and get ready. I've got glue and paint all over my hands and arms." She held out her arms and he nodded when he saw the streaks of paint. "Oregon is teaching me her crafts. I think I won't give up nursing because I'm definitely not crafty."

"Oregon does have a gift," he agreed.

Lilly groaned. "This is painful."

Brody shot her a look and she clamped her lips shut. Next to him, Grace giggled a little. It was a sweet sound. He laughed, because it was contagious.

"She's right," Grace said.

"Yeah, well, don't let her know that."

"At least I lightened the mood in here," Lilly informed them. "You should thank me."

"Thank you, Lilly," Grace responded, and her hand reached for his.

He wasn't sure he felt thankful. Not when her hand on his felt more like her taking hold of his heart.

A few hours later Grace walked toward the back of the rodeo grounds where trucks that pulled horse and livestock trailers were parked. Horses were being saddled, kids were playing in the grass and George Strait played from someone's stereo. Near one familiar trailer, Duke pulled Oregon close and they slow danced, looking very much like a couple in love.

A twinge plucked at her heart. Envy? Because she wanted to be part of a couple. She wanted to do this right, give the baby a family with two parents. She'd been avoiding those thoughts, trying to pretend it didn't matter.

But deep down, it did.

"Hey, there you are." Lilly came out from behind the trailer leading her pretty deep red chestnut horse.

The animal's head lifted, ears twitching as he studied his surroundings.

"He's ready to go," Grace observed.

"Yeah, he knows what this is all about. It's our first year together, but we bought him from a family in San Antonio and their daughter barrel raced."

"I bet you don't often lose," Grace noted, running a hand down the horse's sleek neck.

"Not often, but Dad tells me not to get arrogant. Everyone loses. Play fair and always be happy when someone else has a chance to win." She repeated what she'd probably been told more than once.

"That's good advice."

"Yeah." Lilly grinned. "But I still like to win."

"Don't we all," Brody said as he joined them. "Tie him up and go grab a burger."

"I'm not…"

He pointed at her, and Lilly tied the horse to the side of the trailer. Grace watched as the girl ran off, joining friends as they headed for the concession stand.

"Are you hungry?" Brody offered.

"No. I ate before I left." She looked around, unsure of what to say now. She could tell him she didn't like the distance between them, going days without seeing him. But that was too dangerous. It meant something, this attachment to him.

"Are you hungry?" she asked, because she couldn't think of anything better to say.

"Not really."

She sat down on the tailgate of the truck and he sat next to her, stretching long legs clad in faded jeans. The sun was still hovering on the western horizon and the air had cooled to a somewhat comfortable eighty degrees. She breathed in, relaxing next to his quiet presence.

"How have you been feeling?" she asked when he shifted, bending his knee a couple of times before straightening his leg again.

"I'm good. Better. I shouldn't have put off going to the doctor for as long as I did."

"We all do it. I have an appointment at the end of next week. But Monday I'm going to Fort Worth."

"You're making the drive to Fort Worth? Are you going to the doctor there, too?"

Was that concern in his voice? She glanced at him, saw the tight lines of his mouth and the way his blue eyes focused on the distant hills and not on her.

"I thought I should see my grandparents. They're back this weekend. And I need to go home eventually. At this point I'm the uninvited guest who hasn't left."

"I don't think anyone is in a hurry for you to go home."

She reached for his hand, holding it tight and raising it to kiss his knuckles. "Sweet of you to say, but I know that my presence here hasn't been easy, and I know that Lilly wants her room back. She took one of her posters to Oregon's room because she missed it."

He smiled at her, and she reveled in it, in the way it shifted the handsome features of his face, made him more accessible, more the man she'd known a year ago. She missed that man, her friend.

She wouldn't hurt him again.

"Lilly likes having you around. It gives her something to…"

Grace waited for him to finish but she already knew

the way the sentence ended. "Something to pester you about?"

"Yeah, pretty much. I need to go check on the steers in the pen. Want to walk with me?"

"Sure." She hopped down off the tailgate of the truck and didn't reach for his hand. As much as this felt like their time together last summer, it wasn't.

Sometimes she couldn't remember why she'd broken up with him. Because she liked him too much? Or he liked her too much? It didn't matter. Not now.

They walked together, not touching, past horse trailers, past people she barely knew but Brody had grown up around. She saw Duke on his big gray gelding, leaning down to pull Oregon into the saddle with him.

Brody stopped at a pen holding a half dozen steers. He leaned against the metal rails of the enclosure and Grace leaned in next to him, resting her arms on the cold metal.

Finally she asked the question she'd been putting off. "Brody, will you go with me to Fort Worth?" She didn't look at him. Instead, she watched the steers circling the enclosure, pushing at one another, pawing the dry earth. Restless. She knew how they felt.

They wanted freedom. They wanted out of this pen where everyone watched. They wanted wide-open spaces, far away from the plans that had been made for them.

"Do you need me to drive you?" His voice was low, curious.

"No, but you need to go. Brody, I want you to see your mom. We could make a side trip to Dallas."

He backed away from her, away from the pen. Grace looked at him and he shook his head, repositioning his hat and then turning to land that steady blue gaze on her. "I don't think so. I'll take you, but I don't have a reason to see Sylvia Martin."

"Yes, you do." She reached for him, tugging at his shirt sleeve and pulling him close. "You have to face her with the questions you've wanted to ask."

"I should confront a woman who probably doesn't remember me?"

"You don't know that."

He shook off her hand and started to walk away. She remained next to his side as he headed for his truck and trailer. "Brody, there's a chance she will know you. Does it really matter? You need to see her, whether she knows you or not."

"I don't think so, Grace. I'm pretty good at letting go of the people who don't want to be in my life."

The words hit hard and she stopped walking, stopped following after him. He didn't seem to care. But she did. Her heart broke for him, and with him and maybe because of him.

She wanted him happy. She wanted him whole. She wanted him in her life. She froze at that thought, that unbidden, unacceptable thought.

Chapter Ten

Brody knocked on the door to Oregon's house at 7:00 a.m. Monday morning. Inside he heard Oregon tell him to come on in. For a second he thought maybe he would change his mind. That he'd get back in his truck and they'd never know it had been him at the door.

Before he could make that great escape, the door opened and Oregon gave him a long, steady look. She pushed open the storm door, forcing him off the front stoop.

"You coming in?"

"I considered leaving. But here I am, all dressed up and nowhere to go."

She swept her gaze over his new jeans, plaid shirt and best boots. "You're wearing a knee brace."

"That's the first thing you notice?"

"Yeah, sorry. You do look nice, but you're not the Martin brother I'm interested in, so basically you just look like a cleaned-up cowboy who happens to be chasing after someone else."

"I'm not chasing anyone. And I'm using the knee

brace until I have surgery to clean up the cartilage in my knee."

"I didn't know you were having another surgery or that you'd been to the doctor again," she said as she motioned him in. "Come on in. I have coffee. And Grace, whom I'm sure is the person you're here to see, is getting ready to go to Fort Worth."

"Yeah, I'm going to drive her."

"Oh, she must not know that. She had me take her to get her car out of Jake's garage. She figures it's safe to drive it now that Lincoln is locked up." Oregon poured him a cup of coffee and he took a seat at the table in the center of the kitchen "So about this surgery?"

"I went to the doctor last week and they've decided to do surgery. No big deal. It's outpatient. He said I can probably drive myself home."

"When?"

"I'm not going to have it done until January. I have a lot going on between now and then. We're doing a charity drive for Christmas, and I have some meetings with state workers about the horse camp."

"Brody, that camp is going to be a great thing. Have you ever thought that it could turn into more than just a day camp? With cabins and workers, you could let kids stay on the ranch for a few days."

"I've thought about it. That's in the five-year plan."

Footsteps in the hall ended the conversation. He stood when Grace entered the kitchen. For some reason he couldn't speak. He felt as if he was sixteen again, when Lacy Dodson had asked to sit next to him at lunch. He hadn't believed life could be so good.

She hadn't wanted him for long, either. The memory brought him back down to earth. He cleared his throat and managed to be a grown man.

Barely.

"I thought I'd drive you to Fort Worth to see your grandparents."

"You don't have to." She smoothed her hands down the sides of the floral dress she wore. It looked like one from Oregon's shop—a combination of peasant-style and 1960s hippie. He didn't know much about fashion, but he knew that this style softened the woman who could be a hard-as-nails cowgirl into a woman who looked easy to hold. It hugged her rounded form. It brought color to her cheeks. Somehow it made her brown eyes the color of chocolate and her hair the color of moonlight.

He let out a sigh because those thoughts, about moonlight hair and chocolate eyes, proved that a woman could make a man lose his mind.

"I know I don't have to drive you. But I'm going there anyway, so you might as well ride with me."

"You're going?" She said it sweetly, getting what he meant. "I'm so glad you've decided to do this, Brody. You'll be glad, too."

"I've thought about it." He cleared his throat, looking down at the tile floor. "And praycd about it."

"Then, we should go," she said, plucking at his sleeve, holding the fabric between her fingers. "Before you change your mind."

"I'm not changing my mind," he insisted. He'd been the one pushing this, wanting to know where Sylvia Martin was. Now that he knew, he was going to face her.

"You're not the only one who has something to face,"

Grace told him as they headed down the road a few minutes later. "I have to face myself and my grandparents. I have to face God with the horrible mess I've made of my life."

"I think you've done that already."

"Yes, maybe God, but my grandfather is another matter altogether," she said with a teasing tilt of her lips.

Brody eased onto the main road. "I look forward to meeting him," he said.

She laughed at that. "He isn't as bad as I make him sound."

"I'm sure he's not. As a matter of fact, I think we'll see him first."

"That isn't fair," Grace protested. "You should let me go last."

"No, this trip is yours. I'm just along for the ride, remember?"

She rolled her eyes and reached for the radio. Brody felt the tension breaking free inside him. He knew it would rebuild later, when he faced Sylvia. For now he could pretend they were on a nice country drive, headed anywhere but to their respective fates.

The big house loomed ahead of them. Grace felt everything inside her tense. "This is it."

"It isn't the inquisition or a firing squad," Brody reassured her, reaching for her hand.

"No, it isn't. I know my grandparents love me, so this isn't really about them. It's more about me. It's about facing my mistakes and not hiding from them."

"What would we learn if we were perfect, Gracie?"

She reached for her door as he parked. "I like when

you call me Gracie. It's as if I'm still that person. And you, Brody, you've always known who you are."

"I think you know who you are, Grace," he assured her. "I think you just had to take a detour on the journey. If you'd stayed here, you would have always wondered."

"But the baby, this poor baby didn't ask for all this."

He shook his head. "What, to be born to a mom who will love him and take care of him?"

"But he won't have…" Her baby wouldn't have a father.

"He'll have everything."

She stepped out of the truck. "She."

They walked to the front door of the house and she hesitated before hitting the doorbell. Brody pushed it. Twice. His hand rested on the small of her back, comforting her even if it was meant to hold her in place.

The door opened and her grandmother blinked a few times before her lips turned in a blinding smile.

"Grace, honey. Since when do you ring the bell?" her grandmother admonished as she glanced from Grace to Brody. "And who is your friend?"

"This is Brody. I've been staying with his soon-to-be sister-in-law. Brody, this is my grandmother, Betty Thomas."

"Well, come in, both of you. We were just getting ready to have lunch. Your grandfather has to visit a few church members this afternoon, but he's going to be so glad to see you. And your mom sent a necklace back for you. It's beautiful. The beads are hand painted."

The conversation continued in an easy way as they walked through the house to the kitchen and breakfast nook, where Grace's grandfather was fixing a sandwich. When he saw Grace, his eyes widened. He put down the knife and rounded the counter to take her in a hug.

"My Gracie girl. Where have you been keeping yourself?"

"Granddad, I've missed you."

"We've missed you, too. It's been too long."

"I know, and I'm sorry." She leaned against his shoulder.

He held her away from him, his gaze sweeping, acknowledging and then he hugged her again. "This isn't something you can't get through, Gracie. You're made of strong stuff and that little baby of yours is going to be loved. And you're loved. Isn't that where all things begin, with love?"

"Yes, Granddad, but…"

"But nothing. You made a mistake. If you were the first person to make a mistake, that would be newsworthy. Is this how I wanted things to go for your life? No, probably not. After all, we're grandparents and we wanted the fairy tale for our granddaughter. But this is your story to write, and this is the chapter where you learn lessons about yourself."

Her grandmother put plates, bread, lunch meat and a tray of fruit on the counter. "And what you do next matters."

"I'm going back to college and I'm going to get my nursing degree." She put bread on two plates. One for herself and one for Brody, who stood on the other side of the island, watching out the French doors. "I'll probably move home soon."

Her grandmother circled an arm around Grace's

waist. "Now that we're home, you could come home tomorrow."

"Yes, I could. I just…" She glanced at Brody. He'd turned from the window and their gazes locked. "I've thought about staying in Martin's Crossing. I enjoy small towns."

"I can understand that," her granddad said as his attention drifted to Brody. "You're a Martin?"

"Yes, sir." Brody held out his hand to her grandfather. "Brody Martin."

"It's good to meet you, Brody. I'm Howard Thomas. We're grateful to you and your family for looking out for Gracie."

"We were happy to do it."

Grace pushed the sandwich with a helping of fruit across the counter to Brody. "Sandwich, Sir Galahad."

He arched a brow and took the plate. "Don't mind if I do."

She joined him and her grandparents at the table where they held hands and her grandfather said a blessing. They ate, their conversation focusing on her parents in South America and the short mission trip her grandparents had taken. At one point she thought her grandfather might bring up what happened with Lincoln, but her grandmother shot him a warning look and suddenly he shifted the conversation to the weather.

After they ate, Grace's grandmother took her for a walk. They exited through the side door of the house hand in hand, her grandmother cautious on the stone steps that she'd fallen on the previous year.

"Nan, before you say it," Grace started to say as they stopped at the edge of the patio. "Before you tell me that God has forgiven me, I just want you to know how sorry I am."

"Grace, what I don't understand is why you keep apologizing to us?"

"I'm not sure. I guess I feel as if I've let my family down. I've let myself down. I've let God down. There is a long list of people I've hurt." Including Brody, but she left him off the list. "Apologizing seems to be something I do a lot of these days."

"Well, stop. You've apologized enough, and now it's time to make a plan and move forward. What we've learned in ministry is that when people feel like they've failed, they tend to get stuck in the mistake and dwell in it. Every day becomes about that wrong choice or mistake. They relive it. They repeat it. Start with action. Pick a goal that you can achieve and move forward with a plan that will change things for the better."

"I can do that," she assured her grandmother.

Her grandmother guided her forward. They were heading toward the vegetable garden, although there wouldn't be much to it this time of year. Her grandmother had grown up on a farm and wanted the connection with her past. She put out a big garden every year and spent weeks canning vegetables for winter. She said it kept her young.

"I blame your aunt for this," her grandmother said as she looked the garden over, reaching to pull a few weeds. "Jacki has always rushed through life and away from God. I know she filled your head with nonsense about your gilded cage, because that's how she felt as a teenager. She felt as if the whole world was watching every move she made. So she made sure they watched."

"Aunt Jacki did encourage me to live a little, but she also warned me to stay away from Lincoln Carter. I tried to break things off." Her hand stole to her belly. She closed her eyes. "When he found out I was pregnant, he tried to make me get an abortion. And when that didn't work, he resorted to violence."

"I'm so sorry we weren't here. I'm also sorry you didn't feel like you could tell us."

"I got away." She took in a deep breath and exhaled slowly, feeling the twinge in her back, the telltale sign of a growing baby. "I got away."

"There is no gilded cage," her grandmother repeated. "Yes, there are expectations. Your parents have them, we have them and I know the church has some. But in the end what matters most is that you have expectations for yourself, and you know you're doing what God called you to do."

Grace hugged her grandmother. "Thank you, Nan."

They broke apart and began their walk again. "About the young man in the house..."

Grace kept a straight face. "He's just a friend."

Her grandmother gave her a pointed look but didn't comment.

"He's helped me through a lot," Grace added.

"I'm glad he was there for you."

So was Grace. It hadn't been easy for him, but she was thankful he'd opened the door and let her in.

She and her grandmother picked the few green beans that still clung to vines. They put them in their pockets the way they'd been doing since Grace was a little girl. Her grandmother found a cantaloupe hiding beneath wide, yellowing leaves and held it out to her. Grace lifted it to her nose and inhaled the earthy sweetness.

"Dessert?" her grandmother asked as they turned and headed back to the house.

"Sounds perfect to me."

"Do you have to leave today?" Nan asked as they neared the house.

Grace nodded. "Yes. Brody is going to visit his mother in a residential facility here. And then we head back."

"She'll come home when she's ready, Bet," Granddad called out from a nearby glider. Sitting next to him was Brody, hat in hand.

Grace held her grandmother's arm as they approached the men. Brody stood, pushing his hat back on his head. She was struck by his presence, by her reaction to him being there, in her world. She had two worlds, she realized. She always had. She had lived in this world of privilege, but her heart had yearned for something else, something more basic. Her gaze connected with Brody's and her heart answered the questions for her, what it was she'd been looking for, what she'd been missing.

If only the answer had come sooner. If only she'd recognized it earlier.

"Grace?" Brody's voice eased into her thoughts.

"I'm sorry. I got a little lost in thought. We should go."

"So soon?" her grandmother asked. When Grace nodded, Nan continued, "Then, come home soon. If not, we're going to drive down there to see you."

"We can do both, Nan." Grace hugged her grand-mother. She hugged her grandfather. "I love you."

With goodbyes said, she turned to Brody. "Ready to go?"

His expression altered but he nodded. "Ready as I'll ever be."

They left, walking together to the truck, the heat of late September beating down on them. In the distance she heard the drone of traffic, a jet flying overhead. Familiar sounds. But she'd gotten used to the quiet of Martin's Crossing.

As they headed down the highway, the GPS giving them directions to the facility where Sylvia Martin lived, Grace thought about the past six months.

"I tried breaking things off with Lincoln. More than once."

Brody gave her a quick look, then directed his attention back to the road. "Okay."

"I don't even know why I went out with him."

"He has a way of convincing women that he's charming. From a man's point of view, I can't say that I get it."

"There's nothing charming about Lincoln Carter." She left it at that because now wasn't the time to tell everything about a relationship she should never have started.

The GPS announced there was one mile until their destination would be reached. Grace thought about destinations and where she was going. Her grand-mother had said to pick a goal, something to work toward.

After this, where did she belong?

Chapter Eleven

The facility was long, brick with multiple windows down each side and an entrance in the center. Several people sat under a covered patio. Brody parked, then sat in the truck for a minute looking at the building, not really seeing it. He definitely didn't want to get out and face the woman inside.

"We should go in," Grace said eventually.

Brody nodded, agreeing but not wanting to agree. He'd rather start his truck and head back to Martin's Crossing. He couldn't, though. He'd spent a lot of years wondering where Sylvia had gone and wanting to ask her why she'd left. Today he would face her, but he didn't know if she would remember. He didn't know if she'd be able to answer his questions.

"Let's go," he said, getting out.

Grace walked with him to the front of the building. One of the older men sitting on that patio smiled up at them, and then winked at Grace.

"Thank you, son, for bringing her with you. You just made my day." The old gentleman chuckled and elbowed his friend, who sat next to him in a wheelchair.

The friend glanced up, nodded a little and then dropped his head to resume his nap. The other man shook his head.

"He misses everything. What are you two doing here today?"

"I'm here to see my…to see Sylvia Martin." Brody reached to push the buzzer that would unlock the door and allow them to enter.

"Guess I don't know her. Well, you have a good visit."

Brody opened the door and he and Grace entered the facility with its gold carpet and light brown walls. Once they were inside, he didn't really know what to do. Grace took over, leading him down the hall to the nurse's station. A woman at the desk looked up.

"Can I help you?"

Brody had a lot of answers for that question. Most had to do with why he was here and how he could get out of this mess. He let out a breath and managed to cowboy up.

"I'm here to see Sylvia Martin."

"Are you a relative?" The woman's eyes narrowed as she studied him, then Grace.

"I'm her son."

"I only have one relative listed, a daughter." The woman hit a few buttons on the computer. "Yes, just a daughter."

"I'm not sure why you only have my sister on the list. There are five of us. Well, four now."

"Okay." The woman clicked a few buttons. "I can fix that. Your name is? And can I see ID?"

"Brody Martin." He pulled his wallet from his back pocket. She slid a clipboard across the counter to him.

"Sign here, Brody Martin. I'll walk you down to her room."

"Will she know me?"

She shrugged. "Does she know you? She has some issues but usually remembers people. Kayla was here the other day and she knew her."

"Kayla?"

The nurse cocked her head to the side and looked him over.

"Your sister?"

A small foot made contact with his shin. "Oh, of course."

The nurse gave him a curious look. "Well, let's go see how Sylvia is doing today."

"If you just give me the room number, I'm sure we can find her."

He didn't want this woman to walk with them, to witness his first visit with his mother in over twenty years. He wasn't even sure he wanted Grace with him. But then, he couldn't imagine doing this without her. That was the problem with Grace. He wanted her with him. He wanted her gone. His emotions went back and forth like that about a dozen times a day.

Now, in this moment, he needed her.

The nurse came out from behind the desk. "I don't mind at all."

They walked down a back hall to a room near the end. The door was partially opened, and from inside they heard an afternoon talk show. "She likes her talk shows," the nurse said.

Brody smiled, as if he knew. Because a son should know that about his mother. But he knew nothing about Sylvia, nothing except that she'd left. He should remember more than the bits and pieces of memory he had of her. He remembered decorating a Christmas tree. He remembered church. He remembered her driving away.

The nurse pushed the door open and motioned them inside.

"Sylvia, your son Brody is here to see you."

There was his mother. Brody froze, unsure what to do as he came face-to-face with the woman who had walked out on them. The root of his fears, his obsessions, now sat in front of him. Her dark hair was short. Her eyes were vague and deep set. She studied him as intently as he studied her. And then she cried.

The nurse handed Sylvia a box of tissues. "Sylvia, you never told us you had another child. We only know Kayla."

Sylvia's eyes widened and she looked from Brody to the window. "He doesn't know. No one knows."

"Knows what, honey?" The nurse picked up a blanket and dropped it over the woman in the recliner.

"I wonder if anyone knows where I am?" Sylvia worried her lip as she asked the question. "Where am I?"

"You're in Dallas at the Lakeside Facility."

"I like it here," Sylvia said. And then she looked at Brody again. "How did you find me?"

"Duke found you."

She narrowed her eyes studying his face. "Duke, ridiculous name. Your father picked it. How old are you now?"

"I'll be twenty-seven next week."

"I never liked you boys. Always rough-housing, making messes, dirtying clothes. I hated doing laundry. I didn't like the way you smelled. And your father. I shouldn't have married him. I never did like living in the country."

"Well, let's not beat around the bush," he murmured as she continued to list their sins, the things she didn't like about them.

What had he expected, an apology? Regret? He'd expected her to ask about his life, about her children. He thought maybe she'd be sorry. He should have expected the anger. After all, she'd left and never come back. A person would have to be really angry to make that decision.

He took a deep breath. Right, okay, now what? What was he supposed to say to this woman when it was obvious she didn't want him here, had never wanted him?

A hand touched his back. Sylvia looked past him.

"Who is this? Elizabeth?" Sylvia glared now.

"No, Sylvia, this is a friend of mine. This is Grace."

At that his mother's face fell and one tear streaked down her cheek. "Elizabeth died. I saw it on the news."

Brody reeled. His mother knew. She'd kept track. And she'd never come home. Sympathy and compassion warred with his anger at this woman. If she'd been a stranger, maybe he could have mustered more sympathy. If she hadn't walked out on her children. If she hadn't been the person who left him alone, with scars. Deep-down scars, the kind he'd spent a lifetime dealing with. Scars that had left a little boy crying and a grown man wondering what it was about him that could make even a mother walk away.

"Yes, Elizabeth died. She had two little girls." In the war of emotions, sympathy lost and anger edged ahead. "Our dad is dead, too. I don't know if you knew that. Duke went to Afghanistan, but he came home. If you cared, you'd know that."

"I care." She stood, pushing her frail form out of the chair she sat in. The afghan she'd been covered with dropped to the floor. "I cared. But I wasn't a mother. I was never a good mother. I would have beaten you to death that day if Jake hadn't stopped me."

All of a sudden the memory rushed back, painful and clear in a way it hadn't been all these years. He remembered her hitting him over and over again. He remembered Jake pulling her off him and telling her she wasn't fit to be a mom.

Grace held his hand now, tight. "I'm here," she whispered. He guessed he knew that but he also knew she wouldn't stay long. And he could do this alone. He pulled loose from her and took a few steps toward Sylvia. She looked away from him, but not before he saw her tears.

"You could have come back."

She shook her head. "No, no, I couldn't have. I was having another man's baby."

The words fell into the room and Sylvia fell back into the chair. The nurse told them they'd have to leave. This was enough for today.

Brody stepped away from the nurse. He squatted in front of Sylvia and put a hand on her arm, forcing her attention on him. "Where is she, this sister of mine? Who is she?"

Sylvia shook he head, fast and furious. "No."

"Yes. Tell me. She deserves to know and so do we. She's one of us."

"I can't tell you. I promised not to tell."

"Tell me," he ordered. "Tell me who she is."

Sylvia zipped her lips, as if she was a child locking up her secrets and he was the parent. He turned to the nurse and she shook her head. He started to stand; his knees were burning and he couldn't take much more.

Sylvia's phone was on the table next to her. He pushed himself to his feet and reached for it. Before the nurse could stop him. Before his mother could demand he put it down. He opened the contacts and found the name the nurse had said, Kayla. Kayla Stanford. He pulled out his phone, took a quick photo of the name and number and handed his mother back her phone.

"I will find my sister."

"You shouldn't. She isn't strong. She…she might be like me."

"I don't care. I want to know her."

She stared him down. "Why did you come here?"

"Fool that I am, I wanted to know you, too. I wanted you to tell me why you left. Now I know."

She closed her eyes. "Now you know. And next week, I might not remember." Her eyes opened. "Will you be back?"

Did she want that? He looked at the broken woman sitting frail and forlorn in front of him, and he couldn't be angry. Not the way he wanted to be. Instead, he touched her shoulder. And he forgave her. Or at least he started down that path.

"Yeah, I'll be back."

He walked away, the nurse and Grace following him into the hall. Grace stepped close to him, her hand reaching for his. The nurse walked slightly ahead of him, and if her body language could speak, he guessed she was mad.

"When Ms. Stanford finds out, she's going to be angry. She doesn't like her mother upset."

"Sorry, but I had a right to see her and to know her condition."

"You might have rights, but I have a job to do. I can't let you come in here and upset her."

"It's been twenty years and I had questions. I'm sure you'd have questions, too, if your mother had walked out on you. I'll contact Ms. Stanford myself."

He thought he was doing pretty good until he got in the truck. He sat behind the wheel for a minute, then he brushed at the dampness on his cheeks he hadn't expected to feel. Tears. He was almost twenty-seven and he was crying over Sylvia Martin.

He hadn't cried over her since that first night. Jake hadn't let him. Now he knew why.

"Brody, are you okay?" Grace's voice was soft, sweet. He'd nearly forgotten she was with him.

"I'm good." He leaned back, eyes closed, taking deep breaths to clear the pain that had settled like a rock on his chest. "Man, this is crazy. I didn't remember. I only remembered her driving away and crying because she wouldn't come back. I remembered Duke and Jake holding me back, keeping me from running after her."

"The brain has a way of blocking things."

"Yeah, the painful memories, things that are traumatic. I know. All of these years I remembered her being manic. She would get a little crazy, dancing and laughing. And then she'd get angry. But I never remembered her hitting me."

"I can't imagine."

"I'm glad you can't." He started his truck. "We have a long drive ahead of us."

Before he could shift the truck into gear, she moved closer to him in the seat. With gentle hands she cupped his cheeks and turned him to face her. Her fingers slid through his hair to the back of his head. His heart ached in a whole new way as she touched her lips to his, kissing away the pain.

A whole lot of healing was in that kiss. She timidly brushed her lips against his. And then she leaned in closer. He kissed her back, hungry for her touch, for her kiss.

He needed her. He needed her touch, her softness, her love. He held her close, returning the kiss.

He needed her. But she couldn't fix him. He knew that. It wasn't her place. It wasn't fair to her.

He pulled back, brushing a hand through her hair before setting her away from him.

"That was better than a bandage," he managed to say with a smile.

But it felt a lot like ripping the scab off a wound.

The kiss had scared her senseless. Grace didn't know what to say to him on that long ride back to Martin's Crossing. Even when they stopped to eat, she could only sit across from him and try to make small talk.

Something had come out of that visit, being with him as he faced his mother. She got him now. She understood who he was. Now she got what it meant for him, when he'd picked her, choosing to trust her with his heart.

And she'd tossed it back to him without thinking what it cost him.

He had meant to give her a part of himself, a part

that he'd never given anyone. Now she saw that letting him go might have been the biggest mistake of her life. It was too late for another chance, though. He'd promised never to let her back in. She'd promised her baby that she'd focus on the most important thing in her life—the child she would have in a matter of months.

She must have dozed off, because she woke with a start as he stopped in front of Oregon's place. Her temporary home. She realized that more than ever. Being back in Fort Worth, back with her grandparents, she'd realized that she would have to go back now. There were no more reasons to stay away. She would go back to school, become a nurse, have her baby, and someday she'd have the husband, the home in the subdivision. The way she'd always planned, just with a side trip.

"You okay?" Brody asked as he opened his truck door.

"I'm good. I'm more worried about you," she admitted. "Why don't you stay for a little while? Have a glass of tea or maybe some cocoa. Oregon always has cocoa. The kind with little marshmallows."

"No, I think I'll pass on the little marshmallows. Don't worry about me, Gracie. I'm used to shaking it off."

"Why? You have family. You have friends."

"I'm good. I really am."

"No one is that good all the time, Brody. No one can go through what you've gone through today and not be a little battered."

"Men don't use words like *battered*," he teased. "I'm good. But I'm man enough to admit I've done a lot of praying during this drive home. I have peace, and that does a lot for a man."

He walked her to the front door. She wanted to hold on to him, tell him she got it, that he was strong. But she wasn't. Not the way he was.

At the door he pulled her to a stop next to him. He leaned down, brushed his cheek against hers. "It's just another chapter in my story. What's the next chapter in yours?"

She leaned into his shoulder and his hand rubbed her back, still holding her close. "I wish I knew."

He grinned. She didn't see it but she heard it when he spoke. "I think you know. Don't be afraid of it, Gracie. Just go for it."

He let her go with a hug and she watched as he limped back to the truck and then drove away. She waited until he was out of sight before she opened the door and went inside. She found Oregon in the kitchen at her sewing machine.

"I thought that might be you," Oregon said without looking up. She wore glasses and her hair was pulled up in a bun. Absently she reached for a cup of tea and took a sip before going back to the seam she was sewing.

Grace poured herself a glass of water and took a seat at the table a short distance away. Oregon studied her from over the top of the glasses and then she pushed them to the top of her head.

"You look beat. Rough day?"

Grace nodded, sipping the water. "Really rough for Brody."

"He saw his mom?"

She nodded, wondering how much of the story to tell. She guessed by the next day they would all know.

"They have a sister," she announced.

"Yes, Samantha. She's at college. I met her briefly this summer."

Something must have shown in Grace's face because Oregon's eyes widened.

"They have another sister," Grace explained. "Sylvia was pregnant when she left."

"Wow. That's huge. And how is Brody taking this?"

"He's Brody. I know it hurts but he isn't going to let it get him down. He wants to know her."

Oregon studied her for a minute, then moved to a chair at the table. "Do you love him?"

Grace closed her eyes and sighed. "Yes, but how do I tell him that? I had my chance and I hurt him. And now I'm having another man's baby. Brody is forgiving, but he isn't going to allow himself to be hurt again."

"No one said he would be hurt again. But don't let go of him, Grace. If you love him, give him a chance, because I know he loved you."

Grace fingered the lace tablecloth and nodded. "Yes, loved, past tense."

"Is love that easily forgotten?"

Grace didn't have an answer for that. She only knew that it would hurt to offer her heart to Brody and have him tell her he wasn't willing to give her another chance. It was easier to tell herself that she had to focus on the baby.

And someday, when life settled down, she'd take time for romance. By then Brody would have moved on. She'd be over him.

She hoped.

Chapter Twelve

Brody walked to Jake's the next morning. He needed the exercise to work out the stiffness and he needed to get some fresh air before confronting his brothers. He knew he'd find both brothers together. They'd bought cattle the day before, all young cows, a few ready to drop calves.

He walked through the open door of the barn and saw them leaning over a tractor part. Both were scratching their fool heads as though they didn't know what to do next. They glanced his way and kept talking.

"What did you do to Old Red?" he asked, referring to the tractor that had been on the place for longer than he'd been alive. It was a death trap, the kind that could roll over if a guy didn't turn the wheel just right.

"Nothing, just trying to see if we can order this part off the internet. No one around here has parts in stock."

"I say take Red to the tractor cemetery and call it good."

Duke shook his head. "That's just cold."

"Yeah, well, Red almost tipped on me a few years ago. We haven't been real close since then."

He pulled his phone out of his pocket and opened the photo of the name and number of their unknown sister. With no explanation he shoved it in front of Jake. "Who is she?"

Jake took the phone, lifted one shoulder in a who-knows manner and handed the phone to Duke. Duke did likewise and handed the phone back to Brody.

"Not a clue," Duke said. He picked up the piece of metal. "You know, I don't even know what this part is. I just know it makes the tractor run."

"She's our sister," Brody blurted out, waiting to see if they were as shocked as he'd been. Both looked at him as if he'd lost his mind. Jake took the phone back and gave it another look.

"What are you talking about?" Duke gave him a careful look and then glanced at the phone Jake held.

"I visited Sylvia and when I got there, the nurse said the only one who ever visited was Sylvia's daughter Kayla. She was surprised that our mother has other children. And I was pretty surprised to learn that Sylvia was pregnant when she left here." He narrowed his gaze at Jake. "Is that something you haven't been telling me? That and the fact that she beat me the day she left."

"You didn't remember the beating, so I didn't think it would be good to bring it up. You were always determined to think she was better than she was." Jake picked up the tractor part and headed for his truck. Brody followed behind him, feeling a lot like the kid who had always tagged along behind his older brothers.

"Did you know she was pregnant?"

Jake put the tractor part in the back of his truck and then faced Brody. Duke had followed them out and he leaned against the side of the truck, arms on the side of the bed.

"No. I didn't know she was pregnant."

"She had an affair," Brody went on, half-mad that his voice shook. "So we have a half sister somewhere in Texas."

"Have you thought to search for her on the internet?" Duke asked with a lazy drawl.

"No, I'm too stupid for that," Brody shot back. Sometimes brothers were more trouble than they were worth. "Yes, I did. Last night I typed her name into the search engine, but I couldn't do it. And I haven't called her. It just seemed like something we should do together.

Jake didn't reply. He rubbed the back of his neck and stared out over fields that had turned brown from heat and lack of rain. In the distance the hills were hazy in the early morning light.

"Let's give her a call. Maybe she knows more about us than we know about her," Duke suggested, stepping away from the truck. "I'll call if you don't want to."

"Be my guest." Jake handed him the phone.

Duke punched in the numbers and then he waited. "Kayla Stanford, this is Duke Martin from the Circle M Ranch at Martin's Crossing. I think we're both acquainted with Sylvia Martin. Please call me back at this number." He recited his own number and handed the phone back to Brody. "It's done. Maybe you can let go of the past, baby brother, and get on with your life."

"I'm not dwelling on the past. I just don't like missing pieces. And I can't believe you don't care that we might have a little sister out there somewhere."

"I care," Duke said with a shrug. "But I've dealt with the past. I've moved on."

Brody couldn't disagree, but he wanted to remind Duke that he'd pretty much drank about ten years of his life away trying to get past what Sylvia had done to them. He hadn't bottled up his anger. He'd unleashed it on the world, living fast and furious at rodeos, then in the army.

Jake had become the family's keeper, too busy for anything other than the ranch, his business and raising his siblings.

Brody shook his head, thinking about the mess they all were. Just because one woman couldn't be a decent mom. His thoughts spun to Samantha, their baby sister, left in the care of a dad who hadn't been able to cope and brothers who hadn't known what to do with her. So they'd shipped her off to boarding school.

He guessed they all were at least semifunctional these days.

"So what now?" Brody said. "Did you need some help out here today?

"Not really. I have the guys handling the new heifers." By guys, Jake meant the two men who worked for the Circle M. "I think they're going to work on the fence after that. I have to go to Austin for a few days for a consulting job with a new company. Breezy and the twins are going with me."

"I can do whatever you need me to do around here. And I have a horse to look at this afternoon. I didn't want to have to feed extra livestock through the winter, but it's a good deal."

"I can't think of anything that needs doing. Go look at the horse," Jake said as he walked away from the truck. "I'm heading to the house to get ready for the trip. Let me know if you hear anything from Kayla Stanford."

"Will do," Duke called out to his retreating back. And then, because things couldn't go the way Brody wanted, Duke zeroed in on him. "And how long is Miss Thomas going to be a resident in Martin's Crossing? She told Oregon she likes it here. She said she should go home, but she's gotten used to small town life."

"I don't have a clue what she plans on doing."

"Maybe you should be more attentive to the lady. You can't catch her with this hard-to-get attitude."

"She very politely turned me loose a year ago and I'm respecting that."

Duke grinned, as though he didn't notice Brody was done with the conversation. "You have heard that women change their minds, right?"

"Yeah, so I've heard. I'm not so inclined." Brody waved goodbye and headed for the trail that led back to his place.

He hadn't made it fifty feet when he heard Duke's phone ring. He spun around, heading back that way before Duke even answered. When he got to the truck where Duke stood, he could see by the expression on his brother's face that Kayla Stanford had returned their call.

The call lasted only a moment. Because Duke was Duke, Brody didn't have a clue how it went. He stood there waiting, leaning against the side of the farm truck. Duke pocketed the phone.

Lilly's dog, Belle, joined them. The animal sat at Brody's feet, leaning on his legs, tongue hanging and a dog grin on her face, because Belle didn't have a care in the world other than herding cattle and spending time with Lilly. Oh, and making sure her dog dish was full.

"She's our sister, all right," Duke finally spoke. "She's also the daughter of a lawyer in Austin. I've heard of the guy. He's well-known and political. And Miss Stanford sounds like trouble with a capital T."

"Why do you say that?" Brody absently reached to pet Belle. The dog took a loving swipe at his hand with her tongue.

Duke scratched his scruffy chin. "Well, she said her daddy sure is going to enjoy this scandal. He's getting ready to run for office in a year or so and he'd like to keep family secrets hidden. I got the opinion she didn't much care."

"Great. Another Samantha."

Duke laughed. "Sounds that way. She said she has to work but she'll head this way in a few days. She can't wait to meet us. And her dad never married Sylvia. Seems that Sylvia realized she wasn't much of a mom, so when Kayla was born, she dumped the baby with her daddy and Sylvia skated out of town."

Brody shook his head, half mad, half sad for their mother, for Kayla Stanford and for anyone else left in the wake of the tornado that was Sylvia Martin. A part of him realized she probably couldn't help it. He made the mistake of voicing that opinion. Duke shook his head.

"Don't make excuses for her," Duke said with more

anger than Brody had heard in his brother's voice in a long time.

"I'm stating a fact. She's not a healthy woman, and she probably did the best thing when she left."

"That's generous of you, Brody. But you don't remember what she did to you that day. I can't forget the marks she left on you."

"Maybe you should fill me in."

"You had black marks across your back, bruises on your face. I think she might have killed you for bringing that kitten in the house if me and Jake hadn't pulled her off you. She hated cats."

Brody didn't remember.

"I guess that explains some things." Brody finally edged the words out. "If there's nothing else to do, I'm going to head over and look at that gelding."

"Go ahead. And, Brody, it really is good to forgive. It's the right thing to do."

Brody nodded as he walked away. His phone had been ringing silently in his shirt pocket. He saw that it was Grace. He whistled for Belle to follow and headed down the trail in the direction of Oregon's.

As he walked he realized he was losing the battle—the one in which he kept his heart from getting all tangled up with hers a second time. Knowing that should have been enough to send him back to his trailer.

Instead, he kept walking on the path to Grace.

As Grace poured herself a glass of juice, someone knocked on the front door. She hadn't heard a car pull up, but still she went to the window, her heart racing, worrying that it might be Lincoln.

She really thought she'd shaken her fears, but they

came back at odd times. Especially now, knowing he'd bailed out of jail. Even with the restraining order Jake's attorney had procured, she knew Lincoln could crash into her life again. It seemed she'd spent the past year afraid of being near him, afraid to turn him down. Afraid of what he'd do to her baby.

"Grace, it's Brody."

She relaxed, exhaling the breath she'd held. "Coming."

He stood on the front stoop, cautious, handsome, that one dimple deepening as he flashed white teeth. The bent-up cowboy hat covered his head, but stray curls brushed the collar of his shirt. His blue eyes were dark and lingered on her face.

"I didn't expect you." Did she sound breathless, happy to see him? It hadn't been her intention. But she was—happy, relieved and other emotions that she didn't want to acknowledge. Complicated emotions that she knew would make decisions more difficult.

Stay or go. These days the two choices were constantly nagging at her.

"Didn't you expect me? You called," he teased as he entered the house. "Is there coffee?"

"Afraid not. I could pour you a glass of orange juice." She held up the glass of juice.

"Afraid not." He headed for the kitchen. "I'll make the coffee. Have you eaten anything?"

"I had toast. Brody, you don't have to make me breakfast. I can cook."

He stopped at the door of the kitchen and glanced back at her. "Yeah, I know you can. I also know you probably won't."

"Toast settles my stomach."

"Of course, okay." He rubbed a hand along his jaw and studied her. "I have to go look at a horse I might buy. Do you want to go?"

She wanted to, yes, more than anything. But she shouldn't. But she didn't have plans, nothing to do. It felt as if her life was hovering in limbo, waiting for her to choose door number one or door number two. She wanted another option.

Yes, she'd been praying. Praying and seeking and waiting. And it felt as if answers were still just out of reach.

"Well?" He lifted the empty coffeepot, then returned it to the burner. "Forget coffee."

"I told you there wasn't any."

"I know. Do you want to go?"

"Let me get my shoes." She gave him one last look as she left the kitchen. He was standing at the sink, and he saluted by tipping the brim of his hat and nodding.

Her heart tripped all over itself. That gesture, the man, it was all too much. He was strong. He was vulnerable. He wasn't always as sure of himself as he pretended to be. He had her heart in a way she hadn't expected.

They left a few minutes later, walking the short distance to his trailer, where he'd left his truck. He seemed to be having less pain than he had just weeks ago. She started to mention it but thought better of it. He probably didn't want it pointed out.

"Where did you say we're going?" she asked as she got in the truck.

"The Rockhurst ranch. It's about fifteen miles from here. They have a gelding they want to donate." He closed the door and got in on the other side. "How are you feeling?"

"Good. The nausea is almost gone." She took the opening. "And you?"

He shrugged. "I guess I'm fine. Duke called our sister Kayla. She's going to visit us."

"It's a lot, Brody. Having a new family, finding your mom. On top of…" she didn't finish.

"The arthritis," he finished for her.

"Yes, I guess."

"It isn't a year I'd like to relive," he admitted.

She wondered if he would include her in that sentiment. If he had it to do over again, would he wish he'd never met her? It made her think about what she would change about this year.

She would have turned down Lincoln. She would have been stronger. Her hand stole to her belly because it was a hard thing to settle in her mind. She wouldn't want a do-over with Lincoln. But this baby? She closed her eyes. Maybe she hadn't planned on having a baby right now, but she was, and she loved the little person growing inside her.

One choice led to another. To regret one meant to regret the other. What she regretted was Lincoln. She regretted losing herself, her faith, her convictions. She regretted mistakes made. She wouldn't let her child grow up feeling like one of her regrets.

"It isn't easy, is it, Brody? Everyone says they would like a second chance to do something different. But when we break it all down, thinking about the lessons we've learned, the good things that came from those decisions, it's hard to say we would do something different. I know people would judge me for saying that, but I love this baby. She isn't here yet, but I love her and will love her."

"I know you do," he replied quietly, his tone telling her it was okay.

"I regret hurting you. I regret so much. But I don't regret keeping this baby."

He reached for her hand and she let their fingers touch briefly before his hand returned to the steering wheel.

Silence settled between them until they reached the Rockhurst ranch. It was a pretty place with rolling fields, a creek rushing through a rocky bed and hills in the distance. Horses grazed in a field fenced with white vinyl fencing.

They pulled up to a brick house, long and low, with a truck parked out front.

The owner of the place met them as they walked toward the barn. He was older, with thinning gray hair but a still-handsome face.

"Brody, glad you could make it out here today. This gelding is a good little horse. He's taught several grandkids how to stay in the saddle."

"I wouldn't expect anything but the best from you, Jim." Brody turned to wait for her. She caught up and his arm slipped around her waist, feeling protective. "Have you met Grace Thomas?"

"I think we met at a rodeo last summer. You were with Jacki Thomas?"

"Yes, sir, my aunt."

"I thought so," he grinned. "Jacki is quite a lady. I argued with her once. It only took the once for me to realize I wouldn't win."

At that Grace smiled. "I've had that same experience."

He led them to the barn. "I put Earl Grey in here last night."

Brody laughed a little. "Earl Grey?"

"Don't blame me. The wife likes tea and she named him when he was a foal."

He opened the stall door and Brody stepped inside. Grace watched as he ran a hand over the sleek neck of the dark gray horse. He rubbed the same hand down the horse's legs, checking his hooves, then ran a hand across his back. He stepped around the back of the horse, patting his rump as he moved on to the other side. Grace leaned against the post of the stall as the inspection continued.

"I can't imagine you wanting to give him up, Jim." Brody stepped out of the stall and closed the door.

"Brody, this horse is a special animal. He just seems to get people. If you put a kid on him, he adjusts his entire temperament for that child. He takes care of them. If you're going to start this camp, I want you to start with horses you can trust. And my grandkids have moved on. Either they needed more horse or they stopped riding altogether."

Grace thought she saw a shimmer of moisture in Brody's eyes, but she wouldn't mention it. He reached out and clasped the other man's hand.

"I'll take him, Jim. And I'll take good care of him."

The rancher nodded. "I know that, or I wouldn't have offered. My only stipulation is that if you decide to end the camp, Earl comes back to us."

"I'll put it in writing."

Jim Rockhurst shook his head. "No need. I trust your word."

The two shook hands again. "I'll pick him up tomorrow."

"I'll have him ready to go. And I'll make the missus stay inside so she doesn't chase you down the drive. She loves the idea of giving him to you, but she's going to miss him something awful."

"She can visit anytime. She can even volunteer and help out if she'd like."

Jim walked them back to Brody's truck. "I know she'd like that."

On the drive home Grace realized she would miss out. If she left Martin's Crossing, she wouldn't see this camp or meet the kids who would have their lives touched by an idea Brody had dreamed up and was bringing to fruition.

"You're awfully quiet over there," Brody said as they drove through Martin's Crossing. "Are you up for lunch at Duke's?"

"I would like lunch. And I was thinking that this camp is going to be a great thing and I'd like to be involved."

"Say the word and I'll find something for you to do."

She wanted him to ask her to stay, to tell her she had a place in his life. But she couldn't do that to him. She was going to have a baby who belonged to a man who had been his best friend. She'd made a lot of mistakes, but she wouldn't hurt this man in that way.

Chapter Thirteen

Brody parked his truck behind the church on Wednesday night. He sat there for a long time, almost talking himself out of going inside. In the end he tossed his hat on the seat, brushed a hand through his hair and eased gingerly out of the truck. He headed for the back door, one careful step at a time. This was the consequence of overdoing it. That would be the chapter heading if he was writing a book on rheumatoid arthritis.

He grabbed the rail of the steps and managed, because that was what he did. He bundled up the pain, disposed of it and moved on.

As he walked through the classrooms toward the sanctuary, Lilly came out of the youth room and zeroed in on him the way she'd been doing for a year. Got to love this kid, he decided. She was loyal, unshakably loyal.

"Brody, you are in big, big trouble." She gave him the once-over and shook her head. "What's up?"

"Nothing much. And why am I in big, big trouble?"

"Grace was trying to call you and she was worried."

"Thought I'd dropped off the face of the earth, did

she?" He eased on down the hall, his niece following close by.

"Kind of. She really was worried."

"I'm sure she was, but I'm here now." He didn't know how to tell his twelve-year-old niece it had been a long time since he'd been accountable to someone for his whereabouts.

He'd save that for Grace.

"I've got to get back to class," Lilly hedged, still eyeing him. "You know, you could have let someone know where you were."

"Got it. Next time, let someone know."

"Right." Off she went to storm some other unsuspecting person's life.

The next person he bumped into, literally, was Grace. She came out the door of the sanctuary as he was going in. He touched her arm and then the wall as pain shot down his leg. It took everything he had not to groan. Grace reached out, restoring him to rights, and gave him the once-over, head to toe. "Are you okay?"

"I'm great."

"I was worried about you."

"I went to see Sylvia again. And now I'd like to go sit down."

"I'll go with you."

"Bible study is starting," he noted, heading into the room and knowing everyone was watching. He took the first pew, where they could look at his back and wonder. Grace slid in next to him.

"But you're okay?"

"I might have overdone it yesterday with all the walking. I woke up this morning and my knees were pretty swollen and stiff. I guess the drive to Fort Worth and back didn't help."

"I'm sure it didn't." She sat quietly for a minute, then her hand touched his arm, tweaked the sleeve of his shirt.

He chanced a look at her and found her serious brown eyes studying his face. It shook things loose inside him. And it anchored him. To her.

This was how it felt to have someone. It felt like sitting next to this woman, knowing she cared. She didn't have to touch him. She didn't have to say anything. She just had to be there to make his world a little more right than it ever had been.

And that scared the daylights out of him.

The Bible study started and he focused on the lesson, the discussion and not the confusion that was making him question what he had with Grace Thomas. When her hand reached for his during the closing prayer, he handled it.

"I'll walk out with you. Oregon is parked out back, too."

He looked down at Grace, at her upturned face, her sweet smile. She didn't seem in the mood to back down, not if that glint in her dark brown eyes meant anything.

If he was being honest, he wasn't quite ready to let go of her. It had been a long day. He'd sat with Sylvia and she hadn't remembered him. For a short time she'd thought he was his father. In the end she'd ordered him out of her room.

"Brody?"

"If you're going that way, we might as well walk together."

They took the long walk through the church slowly. He despised weakness. He hated that his body had betrayed him. The grinding in his left knee, even with the brace, was proof that he'd messed up in a big way.

They reached the back door and stepped outside. The full moon shone down, casting a ribbon of silver across the lawn. Cool air brushed over them. Brody breathed in and reached for the hand of the woman on his left. She walked with him down the steps and across the parking lot to his truck.

When they stopped he leaned against the truck, watching her in the pale moonlight. He wasn't ready to let this moment end. And he knew all their moments were ending. He knew that the way he knew that his body was betraying him. Who wanted a broken-down cowboy? What in the world did he have to offer? A single-wide trailer, a lifetime of fighting a disease and some family issues that could make a great reality show?

She gasped, startling him.

"What's wrong?"

He glanced down, expecting a frown. Instead, her mouth widened in an O and then spread to form a smile that touched her eyes.

"She kicked," she said in an awed tone.

"Did she?" He watched as her hand stole to her belly, resting lightly.

"Yes," she insisted. "Brody, she's kicking. You have to feel."

"I don't think…"

She wouldn't take no for an answer. She grabbed his hand and placed it where hers had been, holding it there. "Wait for it."

And then he felt it, that tiny thump as a little foot engaged. He held his hand there a few seconds longer and then he pulled away, because it wasn't his moment. But deep down, he wanted it to be his. He wanted to have the right to stand there with her, sharing all the moments that would matter.

"Thank you," he said as he moved back, putting space between them.

Her hand stole to his cheek, brushing across his jaw and then down to his shoulder.

"You're a good man. Maybe the best man I know."

"I'm just a man, Grace. Not the best. Not the worst." But he loved her. Man, he loved her. And given half a chance, he'd cowboy up and be the husband she deserved and the father her little baby needed him to be.

He wanted that place in her life. He wanted it more than he could ever have imagined.

"Kiss me, Brody."

The command was soft and it lured him. He guessed she probably intended that reaction from him. He'd never been one to turn down a woman. He touched his lips to hers, kissing her the way a woman ought to be kissed. She clung to his arms as he leaned against the truck, held her close. He raised his head and, staring into those dark eyes of hers, he got a little bit lost all over again. He brushed his lips against hers one last time, tangled his fingers in blond hair that wrapped like silk around his fingers, capturing him.

"Go home, Grace." He ground out the words as he backed away from her.

She shook her head. "What?"

"Go home to Fort Worth."

"I'm not prepared to let you tell me what to do,

Brody. Especially when just five seconds ago me leaving seemed like the last thing on your mind. So why do you think you have the right to tell me to leave?"

That was a pretty good question, one he didn't have a real answer for. She had to get back to her life, to her family. He had to get control of his life, and that was hard to do with her living just down the road, all blond hair, deep brown eyes and temptation.

"You don't have an answer?"

"No, I guess I don't."

Every now and then when he felt as if he was falling for her all over again, he remembered how it had felt to sit across the table from her with a ring in his pocket as she told him she thought they should see other people. She wasn't ready to get serious. She had a plan that included getting her degree, getting a job at a hospital in Fort Worth and then someday settling down.

"Brody, let me do something for you tonight. I know you're hurting and there's no reason you can't let a friend…"

He put a hand up to stop her. "I'm fine. I got a shot today and it's already starting to help." He bent his knee to prove his point and he immediately regretted the move. She didn't have to know that.

"Yeah, you're fine."

"I'm fine. I'll see you tomorrow."

She nodded and retreated to the sidewalk.

He climbed in his truck and drove away, wishing that he could go back to the woman in his rearview mirror. She stood in the parking lot for a moment, then she joined Oregon at her car.

Knowing his limits, when he got home he parked his truck right in front of his trailer. From inside he heard the dog barking, first in warning and then demanding he get the door open. When he did, Sally ran out, circled his legs and then ran down the steps to do her business in the yard.

"Come inside," Brody left the door open and went in. He poured himself a glass of tea and crashed in his recliner.

The dog raced through the door, then back out again, barking at something before she ran back inside a second time. Brody patted the arm of the chair. "Get up here, you."

Sally jumped on the footstool of the recliner and started licking Brody's boots. "Crazy animal."

The white head cocked to one side and a happy tongue lolled out of the corner of the dog's mouth. Brody reached to run a hand over her head. He closed his eyes, sighed with pure pleasure. Home felt pretty good.

He must have dozed off because he jerked awake when Sally jumped up, barking with fierceness of a German shepherd even as she cowered next to Brody. He'd left the door open. Not a good move. He didn't want to wake up with an armadillo snuffling around inside his house.

"Go back to sleep. It's probably an armadillo."

Sally growled, as vicious as a dust mop could possibly be. And that wasn't very vicious. "Fine, I'll close the door."

He started to push the recliner down when he saw a shadow cross the door. Great. Just what he needed was a prowler tonight. Or Lincoln. He really didn't feel like fighting Lincoln tonight. But he would.

As he started to get up, Grace stepped into view.

* * *

Grace walked up the steps and through the front door of the trailer. She should have thought more clearly about this plan. She'd told Oregon she was going to check on him and Oregon had kept her opinion to herself, only cautioning her to be careful.

"What are you doing here?" Brody was stretched out on the recliner, his dog next to him. The dog's tail wagged now, and it whimpered rather than the high-pitched barking of moments ago.

"I'm here to check on you. Maybe you could be more appreciative."

"You shouldn't have walked down here. I have a phone if you want to check on me."

"Brody, you're the most stubborn man I know."

"Probably." He stretched and groaned.

Grace helped herself to his kitchen, rummaged through the freezer and found bags of peas. She returned, bringing a chair from the dining room table with her. Brody had closed his eyes but he opened them now. Clear blue stared up at her from a face she longed to touch. She wanted to smooth his brow. She wanted to touch the dimple in the smooth plane of his cheek.

She sat the chair next to him and took a seat, settling the bags of peas on his knees. "The cold will help the inflammation."

"So I've been told."

Right, he was a bull rider, a rancher, a man. He knew about ice packs. She was sure he didn't keep frozen peas in the freezer for evening meals. "Of course you know."

"Thank you, Grace." His voice was husky and soft. She avoided looking at him.

"I'll get you another glass of tea and…" She stood, reached for the glass. "Is there anything else?"

"My evening meds are on the counter."

"Gotcha."

Her hands shook as she opened the bottle of pills. Her heart trembled when she sneaked a peek at the man in the chair, his eyes closed. She should go. She shouldn't be here, opening them both up to heartache.

She sat down next to him and held out the glass of water and the pills. "Brody?"

He opened his eyes and smiled. "You're a good nurse."

"I'm not a nurse. Remember, I ran away from responsibility."

"You're running back to it. You'll get there, Gracie."

She hoped he was right.

He took the pills and set the water glass down on the table. His hand reached for hers. "What's up?"

"Nothing, why?"

"Your eyes tell more than you can imagine. What are you afraid of?"

"I'm afraid I can't go back. I'm going to have a baby. Sometimes I can think this belly and the little butterfly flutters in there are something detached from my life. It's a baby, but right now it doesn't always feel real. But in a few months it will be very real. It will be a living, breathing little person who has demands and needs. Right now I'm still thinking about my plans and my dreams. But it'll all change. Every decision I make will be affected by this baby growing inside me."

His thumb brushed the top of her hand, rough but gentle against her skin. "Now I'm afraid."

"Stop. I'm serious."

"I know you are. I know. But you'll do it because you're determined and because that little guy of yours is going to need you."

"Girl."

His hand stilled over hers. "Right, girl. Or maybe both!"

"I'm not having twins. That would be…"

"It happens."

"You're distracting me."

He sighed and slowly lifted her hand to his mouth, kissing lightly before placing her hand back on the arm of the chair. "Yeah, I'm good at that. I'm all smoke and mirrors."

"No, you're not. You're real and genuine and I needed to be here because you're also my friend."

"Yes, I'm your friend." He said it as if it was the worst thing ever. And she didn't want it to be that. "You're going to be afraid, Grace. You're having a baby. A little human being is going to depend on you for everything. That's huge. But it isn't anything you can't do."

"Thank you." She leaned and kissed his cheek. "You're going to be a good dad someday."

"Right, of course I will. Hopefully by the time I have kids I can still teach them to ride their first pony and take them fishing."

"Brody…"

"No, you get your fears. I get to own mine."

"Then, can I say both of our fears are unfounded?"

"You can say that." His dimple appeared. That one, distracting dimple near the left corner of his mouth.

"How are you feeling?" She stood, touching the bags of frozen vegetables and realizing they'd started to thaw. She picked them up and carried them to the kitchen.

"I'm good. Tired."

"I'm leaving, then." She picked up the chair and returned it to the table in the kitchen.

"Alone?" He sat up, no longer groggy. "Grace, you know I can't let you walk back to Oregon's alone."

"I'm a big girl, Brody."

"And I'm still an old-fashioned cowboy." He pushed the footstool down and got up. "I'm going with you."

"I can call you when I get there."

"You want me to sit here and wait for you to call? I don't think so."

They were walking out the door when she spotted the Moses-style walking stick, hand carved, the wood sanded smooth. She grabbed the carved piece of wood that was almost taller than she was. "Is this yours?"

"Yeah, Lefty carved it for me. He said I'd feel more manly using it."

"Can you part the Red Sea with this thing?" She handed it to him and he surprised her by taking it.

"No, but I can kill a snake with it."

The walking stick had a hand grip about two feet down from the top, making it easy to hold on to. She could tell as they walked that he had used it before. It probably helped take pressure off the knee that was quickly losing cartilage.

"When are they going to do your surgery?"

"Not for a while. Eventually I will require a total knee replacement."

"They won't do that until they have to."

"No." He leaned on the stick, taking the uneven ground with slow steps. "I told you I could still cowboy up and take care of a woman."

"I didn't doubt you."

"No?"

They were almost to Oregon's. She stopped, looked up at him. The moonlight sliced rays of light across the field as thin clouds, white in the moonlight, chased one another across the sky.

"Brody, I really made serious mistakes."

"Yeah, well, we can't undo that, can we?" He kept walking. "Grace, not tonight. I don't want to talk about what could have been. This is the reality. We're both living it. I'm not the man you needed, then or now. I had a lot of baggage to work through, and now I have a few added layers. You're trying to figure out your life, how to go back and finish your education, how to be a single mom."

"Not tonight," she repeated. "What you're really saying is not any night."

"Maybe, Grace. Maybe we both need to step back and focus on figuring out what comes next, because adding another person complicates things." He stopped walking and reached down, letting his hand drift through her hair.

She shivered at his touch, closed her eyes. "This feels like goodbye."

"Yeah, it does."

She nodded and walked away from him, knowing he wouldn't follow. She glanced back as she opened the front door of Oregon's and saw him standing in the moonlight. She wanted to go back, to tell him she couldn't do this alone.

But that was part of the problem. She had to do this on her own to prove that she could. To herself.

Chapter Fourteen

Brody was stretched out in a lawn chair, hat pulled low to block the sun from his face and a glass of iced tea in his hand when Duke pulled up the next afternoon. He squinted one eye at the man watching from his truck. Duke shook his head, said something Brody couldn't hear and got out of the truck.

"A man in jeans, a T-shirt and cowboy boots catching a few rays. This is pathetic," Duke spoke as he walked up to him.

"I'm resting. It's what you do when you have an autoimmune disease. Rest, eat healthy and ignore annoying older brothers. So far it isn't working. I don't feel better at all."

Duke pulled up another lawn chair and sat down. Sally barked a few times and jumped on Duke's lap.

"Is this how you've spent your birthday?" Duke asked, his tone saying he wanted to sound as if he didn't care. Brody grinned. Of course his big brother cared.

"Yep" seemed like the best answer.

"Yep? Well, you've got some womenfolk pretty

upset. They're at Jake and Breezy's cooking up something. They want to surprise you. I knew you wouldn't come up even if I begged. So I'm using guilt to get you up there, because I know you don't want to hurt anyone's feelings."

"Nope."

Brody pushed his hat back and zeroed in on Duke. Duke grinned. "So it's working?"

"Yeah, I guess I don't have a choice. I'm twenty-seven. If I could, I'd do a happy dance for you."

"But since you can't, you'll come down to Jake's and eat cake and make as if you're having the time of your life. If you don't, Lilly will be crushed. She made you something special."

"I'd do anything for your daughter, so don't use her that way."

Duke held up his hands in surrender. "Never ever would I use my daughter to manipulate my little brother."

"Thanks. That means a lot to me." He pushed himself up and reached for the walking stick. "I'll be down in an hour. Is that good?"

"It is. Do you want me to wait for you?"

"No, I can manage." He wanted to say more, but he didn't. He knew Duke cared. He cared about Duke. So why fight on his birthday? It just didn't make sense.

He was almost up the steps of the trailer when Duke stopped him, "Hey, Brody."

He turned, waited.

"Oregon said that Grace cried herself to sleep last night. Did you do that?"

Brody rubbed a hand across his jaw. He really

needed to shave. And make things up to Grace. "Yeah, probably," he admitted.

"You should know pregnant women cry a lot. They get their feelings hurt easily."

"How would...?" He stopped himself from saying something about his brother not being there when Oregon was pregnant. "I'll make it up to her."

"That would be real good of you."

Brody leaned against the door frame. "Duke?"

"What?" Duke stood in the yard. Brody's dog was on its hind legs, scratching at his pant legs.

"I wish it was my baby. That makes me madder than anything. When I touched her belly last night and felt that little person in there kick my hand, I wanted that baby to be mine. I'm furious that it's Lincoln's."

"I get that, Brody. I guess you just have to..."

"Pray. Yeah, I know. I've been praying night and day. I'm not sure God is hearing me, because I still don't have an answer. The last time I thought I had an answer, I bought a ring. We all know how that turned out."

"Yeah, we know. It ended with you coming home madder than a bear with a thorn in his paw."

"I'll be down in an hour." He whistled for his dog and went inside to get ready.

When he pulled up to Jake's, there was a full house, and a truck with a snazzy horse trailer parked outside. He knew that trailer. It belonged to Grace's Aunt Jacki. It had living quarters, room for three horses and air conditioning. Not only did Jacki travel in style, but so did her horses.

He headed for the house, stopping to pet Lilly's dog. When he stepped onto the front porch, the door opened.

Grace stood in the doorway, her smile hesitant. She was wearing a pretty skirt and a T-shirt. Her hair was held back from her face and her eyes looked huge. And still a little red. Guilt edged in and he tamped it down.

"How are you?" she asked, protective hand on her belly.

"Is he kicking?"

"No. I'm just a little sore. I have an appointment Monday."

"I'll drive you," he offered, really hoping she'd take him up on it. And then hoping she wouldn't.

"I'll think about it."

"Jacki is here." Needless words. She knew her aunt was there.

"She brought my gelding, Doc. I'm going to keep him here until I decide my next move. I can't stay with Oregon forever."

"She's going to move out soon. You can probably stay there as long as you want."

He felt it between them, the tension, the need to say more. But he wasn't ready. He guessed she wasn't, either. Maybe neither of them knew what it was they wanted to say.

"I'm sorry about last night."

"Who told you?" She joined him on the porch, slowly closing the door behind her.

"Oregon told Duke. He said something to me." He eased closer, inhaled the sweet scent of her perfume. She was springtime and sunshine. He needed her close. He didn't deserve her, though.

"Brody, I'm tired of hurting and it seems as though that's all we do—hurt each other."

The words stunned him. "I don't want to hurt you."

"I know. And I don't want to hurt you, either."

He leaned in close, letting his lips graze her cheek. "I know. I didn't mean to hurt you last night."

She nodded, her forehead touching his chest, resting there. He leaned, kissed the top of her head. "We should go in," he said, regretting that they were here and not somewhere alone where they could talk.

"I know."

He reached for the doorknob, but stopped as a car roared up the drive and pulled in to the parking space behind his truck. The cherry-red convertible blasted rock music. The woman behind the steering wheel had long dark hair pulled back. Sunglasses perched on a pert nose. She stepped out of the car and looked around, and he knew immediately who she was.

"Who invited Kayla Stanford?" he asked as he watched her walk toward the house.

"Is that who that is?"

He watched her head their way. "I'm guessing."

"No one invited her, that I know of. She did say she was going to visit. She seems to know how to make an entrance."

"I'd say so," Brody agreed.

"I think Martin's Crossing is in trouble."

"Is this the Martin ranch?" the young woman asked as she stepped up on the porch, all confidence and style. The kind that came from growing up privileged.

But something in her gray eyes made the outward appearance seem like a lie.

"It sure is," Brody responded, holding out a hand. "Brody Martin."

"Kayla Stanford. I guess you're my brother." She gave him a winning smile and Brody silently agreed with Grace. They were all in big trouble. This young woman in her knee-length yoga pants, T-shirt and designer sunglasses was not at all what they'd expected.

Brody took a few seconds to let it settle in. "I'm not even sure what to say in this situation."

"Yeah, that's how I've been feeling, too," she admitted. "I was led to believe my mother had never been married. She had me, dropped me with my dad and flew the coop."

"She's an expert at flying the coop," Brody informed her. "But not at raising kids."

He led her inside to the rest of the family. Party horns sounded as they headed for the kitchen. He led Grace and Kayla to the big room where the family was gathered. That included Marty, their housekeeper, cook and mother figure. Her eyes widened when she saw Kayla. The horn blowing stopped.

"Happy birthday!" Lilly's greeting fizzled as everyone looked from him to Kayla.

"Surprise!" Brody half shouted and waved his arms. "It's a sister."

Kayla stood in the middle of their rowdy group, chewing on her lip. Brody put a hand on her arm and she half smiled up at him.

"Let me introduce you to everyone," he offered. It never should have been like this. People didn't get introduced to siblings. He couldn't help but be mad at Sylvia all over again. She'd abandoned them all without a thought toward their futures or how they'd find each other.

He had a real feeling that Kayla Stanford had needed to find them. And being the family they were, they pulled her in, talking, asking questions, letting her be part of them.

And standing at the edge of their family was Grace.

"Do you have other family?" Breezy asked later as she served the white cake that looked like a Maltese. He couldn't figure out how they'd all thought he needed a dog cake for his twenty-seventh birthday. There had been years as a kid that he'd been okay with cream-filled snack cakes all lined up in a pan and candles on top. Jake and Elizabeth had made them.

Kayla took a bite of the cake and answered Breezy's question. "My dad, stepmother and two half brothers."

It was something Brody hadn't known about her.

"You have a great car," Lilly observed.

Kayla smiled. "Thank you."

The conversation drifted again. Jake questioned Kayla about school. About how she spent her time. Brody kept quiet because they all knew how she spent her time. Creating headlines in Austin. She was her father's wild child. It was hard to figure that out now that he'd met her.

"I'm going to walk Aunt Jacki out. She's leaving." Grace stood, picking up her empty plate.

Brody took the plate from her hand. "I'll get these."

"You're sweet, Brody."

"Don't let that get out or they'll all start expecting some miraculous transformation," he teased.

She touched his cheek, her fingers barely caressing the skin. "I won't tell."

Why did he have a strange feeling they were close to saying another goodbye?

Grace walked across the yard with her aunt. She'd shown up without notice, but that was okay. Jacki was notorious for drifting whichever way the wind blew.

She was turning forty this year and she said she had a lot of adventures to take before she settled down.

When they got to her truck, Jacki pointed to the open tailgate. "Sit."

Grace obeyed. Jacki sat next to her.

"Why didn't you tell me Lincoln was abusing you?" Jacki started with the conversation that had probably been eating at her all day.

"I don't know." Grace held her hand out to the border collie that had joined them. The dog licked her fingers and then plopped in the shade of the truck, stretching out to sleep. "I guess I was embarrassed. I'm not a woman who gets abused, right? I'm educated. I'm from a good family. It doesn't happen."

Jacki let out a sigh. "Oh, honey, it happens. I was married for two years to a man who thought I was his personal punching bag. I just never saw it in Lincoln, and I'm sorry."

"It wasn't your fault. I'm starting to realize it wasn't mine, either."

"Where is Lincoln?"

"I've heard he's in Montana with an uncle." Grace lifted the hair off the back of her neck. "It's hot."

"No, it isn't. You're pregnant."

"I know." Grace closed her eyes, reliving. "I'm not going to blame Lincoln, but I do blame myself. I should have walked away."

"Grace, it is his fault that he hurt you. I'm sure he tried to tell you that it was your fault, and that you made him do it."

"I know it wasn't my fault. But I'm taking responsibility for my part in this, Aunt Jacki. I made really bad decisions, and I gave up part of myself. Now I have to find who I am again. It's way past time for Grace Thomas to take control of her life and grow up."

"What about that good-looking cowboy in there?" Jacki asked.

"I have to find myself before I let anyone else in my life."

"So should I load that horse up?"

She shook her head. "No, not yet. I talked to Oregon. I'm moving back to the apartment in town. If I go home I know everyone will help me out. They'll take care of me. But I don't want to be taken care of. I've been letting too many people make decisions for me, Aunt Jacki. I went to nursing school because my parents are in the medical field. I went to church because my grandfather is a pastor. I moved in with you because you said—" she reached for her aunt's hand "—I needed adventure. And you were partly right. I did need to find myself. But what I've learned is that I need to make some decisions for myself now."

Her aunt hugged her. "Girl, I am so proud of you. You're going to do great things, no matter what you decide. Just be strong for yourself, for your baby."

She nodded, leaning in to her aunt. "Thanks, Aunt Jacki."

"Well, I should be heading home, then. And you call if you need anything."

"I'll call."

They hugged one last time, then Grace stepped back as Jacki climbed in her truck, gave a wave and headed down the drive and back to Stephenville. When she turned back toward the house, she saw Brody.

"We should talk," he said as she walked up the steps

of the porch. He motioned to the rocking chairs and they sat together.

Grace wanted to reach for his hand but she knew it was the wrong time. "Brody, I'm staying in Martin's Crossing. But I'm staying for me, not us."

"I heard."

"I'm sorry," she whispered, really wishing she could reach for his hand. As much as she needed to be strong, she realized she needed his strength. But that was the problem, wasn't it? She needed to find her own strength, her own way.

"Don't be sorry, Grace. Just be happy. I'll be here if you need me."

"Thank you." She stood and he remained seated. She saw the hurt in his eyes. She wanted to tell him that maybe someday… But she couldn't. She wouldn't make promises she couldn't keep. And she wouldn't keep him tied to her, waiting for something that might not happen.

She needed time to have a baby and focus on herself.

"Grace, remember, if you need anything…"

"I'll call."

He pushed himself up from the chair. "Could you tell them I had to head back to my place? I'm packing today. I'm moving in to Lawson and Elizabeth's house."

"I'll let them know."

He waved as he walked away, not even turning to look back at her. She could handle this. She took a breath and rested a hand on her belly. She had this little person counting on her to be strong and make the right decisions.

All of her life people had counted on her to do the right thing. She'd done her best for all of them. This time it was different. This time it was for her.

But her heart broke a little as she watched a cowboy walk away from her for the second time.

Chapter Fifteen

B rody missed his trailer. It wasn't that Lawson and Elizabeth's house was at all bad. No, it was the opposite of bad. It looked like something out of a magazine. Stone and wood floors, big windows, a kitchen that a man could get lost in, even if he could only cook scrambled eggs. It had a great stable. He guessed the stable was the biggest attraction for a guy wanting to start a riding camp.

As he walked out to that stable on a morning in early November, Sally following, he thought about checking on Grace. But he wouldn't. He saw her from time to time, but he was giving her space. Even though that space left a big hole in him.

At least he knew where she was and that she was safe.

From the field his horse Jaz whinnied. And then Earl Grey took a turn, whinnying and heading toward the fence. Brody waited for the two animals. In the distance he heard a truck. Sally had plopped to the ground next to him but she jumped up and started barking.

"Hush, crazy dog."

A minute later Jake's truck pulled up the drive. Brody shook his head and gave his attention back to the horses. Jaz got to him first, pushing against his hand looking for a treat.

"Sorry, Jaz. I'm out of carrots. I'll get some at the store today." Earl, usually the dominant animal, pushed Jaz away and came in search of a treat. "You two don't give up."

"Hey, how's it going?" Jake walked up, petting Jaz first and then reaching out to Earl. "He's a good-looking horse. Nice of Rockhurst to give him to you."

"Yeah, it was. I have another gelding on the line, too." Brody backed away from the fence and headed toward the barn. He knew Jake would follow. "What brings you out here today?"

"Not much. I have to run to town for antibiotics for some calves and thought I'd stop by and see if you wanted to come over for dinner tonight."

"Sounds good. Scrambled eggs get old after a while. I'd offer to bring something but I'm sure you'd rather I stay out of the kitchen."

"I think we'll be good. Thanks for the help yesterday with that heifer."

They'd had to pull a calf the day before. It hadn't been easy and they'd almost lost the momma in the process.

"That's what I'm here for." Brody waited, because he knew eventually Jake would get around to his real reason for being here.

"Have you talked to Grace lately?" There it was. Jake's reason for showing up. His family had taken to not mentioning Grace. There had to be a good reason for bringing her up now.

"No. I see her at church, and every now and then in town. She's busy taking online classes and getting ready to have a baby."

"Yeah, I know. I guess it probably isn't easy for you that she's having Lincoln's baby."

Brody stepped into the barn, flipping on a light as he went. Jake followed, waiting for an answer. As if Brody had one.

"I guess it doesn't really matter. It isn't my baby and she isn't my concern."

"You know, Joseph had a similar situation with Mary," Jake interjected, as if that made sense.

Brody groaned and put a hand up to stop his brother. "For a smart man you come up with the strangest analogies. Do not even try to compare this to Joseph and Mary."

"I'm just saying you can love a woman and the child she's carrying, even if the child isn't yours. I love Rosie and Violet…"

"We all do. And I love…" He shook his head and walked away. "What do you want?"

"I wanted to tell you that Grace is alone. She's having an ultrasound today and she wouldn't let Oregon go with her."

"Women have ultrasounds all the time. What's so special about this one?"

"She had an appointment last week and they're concerned, so they scheduled an ultrasound."

That stopped him in his tracks. The baby. He still didn't know if it was a boy or a girl. He hadn't asked because it wasn't his business. Now his heart kicked in and he tried to brush it off, to tell himself it wasn't his problem.

"You don't know what they're looking for in the ultrasound?"

"No, I don't. I just thought she shouldn't be alone. Breezy is strong, Brody. She's as independent as a woman comes. But she doesn't like to be alone when she goes to the doctor. I hold her hand every time she has an ultrasound."

"She's your wife. You have that right."

"Guess I'm pushing where it's none of my business."

Brody carried a few flakes of hay to the corral where the horses were waiting for breakfast. "I guess you are. If Grace wanted someone with her, she would have asked."

"You're right." Jake put a booted foot on the bottom rail of the corral.

"I know I'm right. You came out here thinking if you told me she needed someone, I'd go running and suddenly we would be all fixed. We don't need that, Jake."

"What do you need, then?"

"I guess space. And time. Grace has a life to figure out. I have to get this camp organized and horses bought. I have to deal with my health issues. She doesn't need that on top of what she's going through."

"I'm not sure I'm following," Jake said as they turned away from the fence.

"I don't know if you haven't noticed, but I'm having some health issues."

"And you think that's going to be a deal breaker for a woman? Brody, you look for reasons to sabotage relationships."

"Well, I guess I learned from my more experienced older brothers," Brody shot back.

"If you want to learn something from us, learn this before it's too late—don't push away the people that mean something to you."

"I'll take that into consideration."

Jake headed for his truck. "Right, you do that. Take into consideration that someone might need you today."

"I'll take that into consideration, too," he muttered as he walked back down the driveway to the house. The big, lonely house. Yeah, that was what he missed about his trailer. It had been small but it hadn't felt empty.

When Lawton and Elizabeth had been alive, this house had been full of people, full of laughter. Now it was hollow with the distant memory of their family echoing in the halls. Their family pictures were still on the walls. Their things were still in the closets.

A few days ago he'd been going through some stuff in one of the rooms upstairs and he'd found a gift that Elizabeth had bought for Lawton but had never got the chance to give him. He shook his head, remembering how he'd sat there crying over the vinyl records she'd meant for Lawton to add to his collection.

Later he'd gone downstairs and played them on the old record player. He'd sat in the big leather chair in front of the fireplace and listened to George Jones.

This house deserved people. A family.

Not a lonely cowboy who gimped around and wished he had a life.

Brody watched his brother drive away, then he went

inside. He made a few phone calls, put Sally in her kennel and headed out.

Grace might not welcome him at her side, but he'd take his chances. If something was going on, she shouldn't be alone. After all was said and done, if she wanted space, he'd give it to her again.

But today, she wouldn't be alone.

Grace closed her eyes and prayed. Again. She'd prayed a lot in the past few days. She'd prayed for her baby. She'd prayed that she'd have strength to face whatever came her way. She opened her eyes, aware that a few people in the waiting room were watching her. A woman about her age gave her a sympathetic but understanding smile. They were both alone. Grace smiled back, drew in a deep breath and somehow felt a sense of peace that had been evading her. She wasn't alone. Not really.

God would not leave her or forsake her.

The woman sitting opposite her looked toward the door and smiled. Grace glanced that way and for a moment everything went fuzzy. Her eyes filled with tears that she fought back. Brody. Six feet of cowboy and the quiet strength she suddenly needed. He closed the distance between them and took the seat next to hers.

She hadn't wanted anyone here. She had been determined to do this on her own. That suddenly didn't make sense.

"I'm so glad you're here." The words rushed out.

"You should have called. You know I would have driven you. As it is, I had to bring Duke with me to drive your car home. He's waiting outside for your keys."

"You don't have to do that." She brushed a hand across her eyes. "You really didn't have to come."

He picked up her purse. "Find your keys, Gracie."

She nodded and dug through her purse, found the keys and handed them to him. He left her briefly and when he returned to sit next to her, she thought she'd never been so glad to see anyone.

"Thank you." She rested her head on his shoulder.

His arm circled her. "Anytime, Grace."

When they called her name she froze, and the peace she'd been clinging to fled. She didn't want to face this diagnosis. She closed her eyes and Brody's arm tightened around her.

"Grace, whatever it is, I know you can get through this. I know God can get you through it."

She nodded. "You're right. I'm afraid, but I can do this."

"That a girl. And I'll be right here if you need me."

She stood, reaching for her purse. He handed it to her.

"Brody, I need you. With me, back there. Please. I know that's a lot to ask. I know it isn't what you planned. But I can't do this alone."

He went with her. She held on to his hand as the nurse led them to the exam room where they would do the diagnostic ultrasound.

"Go ahead and lie down, Grace." The nurse straightened the paper sheet and pillow. "It isn't comfortable, but it won't take long."

Grace knew it wouldn't take long. In a matter of minutes they would be able to tell her how her life would change. Brody held her hand as she took her place on the exam table. She leaned back, closing her eyes, wishing this moment away and knowing she had to face it.

This was when parenting began, she realized. Long before a baby came into the world, mothers made choices, faced sickness and fought for their child.

The doctor and an ultrasound tech entered the room. Grace smiled at Dr. Patterson. He wasn't a tall man, just a few inches taller than she was. He had sandy-colored hair and an easy smile. She had liked him immediately. And she trusted him.

"Grace, I'm glad you brought someone with you." Dr. Patterson patted her leg. "I know you've probably been worried, but I want you to relax. Take good deep breaths and remember that faith you told me you have. The tests the other day were inconclusive, so we want to take another look at this little person so we can know what we're dealing with."

Grace could only nod. Her hands shook. Her body trembled. She didn't trust that she could open her mouth without her teeth chattering. Dr. Patterson turned up the heat in the room.

The hand holding hers gave a light squeeze, remind her she wasn't alone. She opened her eyes and his gaze held hers. She nodded and just one corner of his mouth tilted up, showing that dimple. She loved that dimple.

Dr. Patterson took the seat where the ultrasound tech should have sat. He squirted gel on her belly and started to roll the ultrasound wand, catching the image and a heartbeat almost immediately. The tech leaned in, watching as he clicked for measurements. Grace looked for something, anything. And then she looked to Brody, catching his lean-cheeked profile as he studied the images in shades of gray and black. Her baby moved, a small hand grasping at nothing, a foot lifting.

"It's a girl, Brody," she whispered. A tear slid down her cheek.

"Are you sure that's not a boy?" he teased.

Dr. Patterson captured a few more images and then hit a button to eject the photos he'd taken. He handed one to Grace. And he smiled. "Nope, that's a girl."

He continued to take photos. He clicked measurements. He sat back and let out a sigh. And then he turned, smiling.

"Grace, I think we're just fine here. There was some concern about head size and growth, but I think your little girl is healthy, and when you hold her in a few months, you'll both be happy."

Hold her. Grace's eyes filled with tears. Happy tears. She would hold her baby. "Thank you." The words came out on a sob. "Thank you."

"You're welcome." He handed her a tissue for her eyes and a towel. "And now I have a baby to deliver. Your little girl is healthy. Schedule your next appointment and I'll see you in a month. Of course, if you have any concerns, call us."

She nodded, watching as he left. The technician followed. She and Brody were alone. She sat up, her legs dangling over the side of the table. Brody was still looking at the picture she'd handed him.

"A girl." He grinned at her. "That's pretty amazing, Gracie."

"I know." She started to hop down from the table. Brody stopped her.

"Shoes?" He picked up her shoes and carefully slid

them on her feet. And then he took her hand and helped her down.

Someday Brody would be someone's husband. He would be a father. Her heart tripped over that thought. She closed her eyes, willed those images, the ones of him in her life, away. It was too easy to visualize him holding a baby girl close. It was too easy to imagine him with her.

Life wasn't that easy.

A few minutes later they walked out of the clinic. Sunshine and blue skies greeted them, always a surprise after being in a windowless office. The air was cool, the way fall air should be.

"How is school going?" Brody asked as they headed for his truck.

"Good. I added some psychology classes. I realized that I love nursing, but I want to make it the career I choose. I'm not sure what the future holds, but I know that there are things I want to do that I hadn't considered before."

"I'm glad to hear that," he said as he opened the truck door for her.

"And you, Brody. How are you doing?"

"Good. I'm in remission. As long as I wear the brace, my knee isn't too bad. And I'm having surgery in January."

He stepped back to close the door.

She stopped him. "Brody, I miss you."

"I miss you, too."

"Do you think…" She sighed. "Do you think we could still be friends?"

He glanced away, leaving her with just the view

of his profile and a jaw that clenched as he studied the horizon.

"We're still friends. That's why I'm here."

She nodded and moved her hand. He closed the truck door.

When they were almost back to Martin's Crossing, Brody pulled into a Western store. He didn't say anything, didn't even invite her to go in with him. He parked, went inside and a moment later returned with a bag. Grace watched him walk down the sidewalk.

He got in, handed her the bag, started the truck and took off down the road again. She sighed, exasperated with his silence. He grinned. "Open it."

So she did. She pulled out a tiny box and took off the lid. Inside she found a pair of the tiniest pink cowgirl boots she'd ever seen. She lifted them out of the box.

"Thank you. They're perfect."

He nodded and kept driving. A couple of sleepless nights caught up with Grace and she dozed, waking when the truck stopped. She opened her eyes and realized they were home. Or she was home. Lights twinkled in Oregon's All Things and only a few cars filled the Main Street parking spaces. Her stomach growled.

"Duke's is still open. Do you want me to bring something over?" Brody offered as he pulled the keys out of the ignition.

"I'd love something to eat." And more time with Brody.

"Go on in and I'll be back with dinner. Do you want the special? I think it's chicken-fried steak."

"That sounds really good. I didn't eat much today."

"No, you probably didn't. I wish you would have called me."

"I wish I had called you, too." The honesty in the statement took her by surprise. It made her think about how different the past few days might have been if she'd had Brody.

But she didn't have him.

Chapter Sixteen

Brody knocked on the door of the apartment and heard a muffled, "Come in." He entered, kicked off his boots and set the food on the table. The room was lit only with a lamp in the corner and a light over the sink. A candle burned, already adding the scent of cinnamon to the air.

Grace was curled up on the couch. She started to get up, but he motioned for her to stay. "I'll bring it to you."

"Brody, you don't have to do that. Honestly, you don't have to be here."

He knew what she wanted to say—his presence complicated things. He complicated their lives by caring. He got it, most of the time. He'd thought about it from her perspective. She'd lived her life for other people. This was her time to find out what she wanted.

"I'm here, Grace." He found a tray in the cabinet, put her food on a plate and carried it to her on the tray, along with a bottle of water.

She sat up and he placed the tray over her lap.

"I'm not sick," she insisted, but weariness settled in her eyes.

"No, but you're worn out and you need energy. That little girl needs you strong." He sat down across from her. "I'm not moving into your life. I know you need space. I'm here because you need someone to take care of you today."

"You're a good someone, Brody." She ate a few bites and stopped. "Aren't you going to eat?"

"I'm not hungry."

She gave him a look, but she didn't argue. He watched as she ate every bite, closing her eyes as she ate the last of the potatoes and then lifted the tray off her lap. He took it, setting it on the coffee table. "I should go. Is there anything else I can get before I leave?"

She shook her head.

"Do you want me to call someone? Your grandmother," he offered.

"Brody, you're the only someone I want. But I can't, not now. I'm learning things about myself that I never knew. Like how much I love psychology. And afternoon talk shows. I don't like contemporary music in church. I love the old hymns. I love our church and the people. I love Duke's chocolate cream pie. I love this town with no stoplights. I don't mind that I can't run to the mall. All of the things I always thought were me aren't me at all."

"You don't have to convince me," he assured her. He didn't know what else to say. Except maybe he wanted to tell her that he didn't ever want her to leave this one-horse town or him.

"I brought you a piece of that pie. It's on the counter," he told her. "And now that you've eaten, I should go."

A smile broke across her face, the first real smile he'd seen there in a while. "And you're just now telling me?"

She jumped up and hurried to the kitchen. He watched as she opened the container with the biggest piece of pie Ned could fit. She grabbed two spoons and joined him in the chair, sitting on the arm and resting against his shoulder. She filled a spoon with pie and shoved it at him. He took a bite and then she handed him the spoon.

"We can share," she offered and took a bite with her own spoon.

"Thanks."

She took another bite, her eyes closing. "I don't know how he does this. It's the best pie ever."

"He says it's all about the type of chocolate. And he won't tell what type that is."

"I wouldn't want to know. I don't like to bake. Another thing I've learned living on my own. I do like to cook, but I'd rather eat pie made by someone else."

"Any other life-changing realizations?" he asked. He wasn't sure if he wanted to hear the answer.

She finished the last bite of pie and took the container, setting it on the table. She turned to face him. Her hands moved to his cheeks and she smiled.

"I like cowboys. I don't want a lawyer or a doctor or a scientist. I want a cowboy who cares about kids."

He closed his eyes and she leaned, kissing him lightly and then whispering, "I want a cowboy."

"Grace, you're killing me."

"I know and I'm sorry. Brody, I'm having a baby.

I'm finishing college. I'm having your best friend's baby. But you're the someone I want."

"He stopped being my best friend a long time ago," he reminded her.

"I know that. It's just always going to be between us, isn't it? This baby is his. I love her and I will always love her. But I can't undo the fact that Lincoln Carter is her father."

"And you thought, what, Grace? That I'd hold it against you? Or against her?"

"I don't know. I only know that I hold it against myself."

He cupped the back of her neck with his hand and pulled her close, touching his lips to hers, melting them together for an achingly brief moment.

"I love your baby girl," he assured her. "When I think of that baby, I think of someone I can't wait to meet and hold. Grace, I want to be a part of her life. I want to be part of your life with her. But I'm not going to push."

"I know you won't. I just wish I could give you more." She caressed his cheek, her fingers brushing along his hairline. "I know it's selfish of me, but don't give up on me. Please."

"I don't give up easily." He closed his eyes and then shook off the web of emotions that held him captive. He stood, pulled her to her feet with him. "But I have to go."

"I know."

"Make me a promise, Grace." He led her to the door with him, not wanting to let her go just yet.

"What's that?"

"Don't go through something like that alone. Next time, call me."

They were at the door and she leaned, resting her head on his chest. She had to hear his heartbeat racing. It was chasing after something he didn't know he would ever have.

"Next time I'll call." Her hand rested on his chest and once again she found the chain. "You're wearing it again."

"When I was packing up I found it on the counter of the trailer. I decided the safest place for it is around my neck."

He'd much rather have it on her finger. But he couldn't say that.

Not yet.

Grace pulled the chain free from his shirt and held the ring in her hand. The metal was smooth and cool; the diamond sparkled in the dim light of the room. The silver cross hanging with the ring was warm from being against his body.

Brody pulled the chain off his neck and raised it to her head. Her heart stilled as he dropped that chain over her head, settling it into place around her neck.

"Brody?"

"For safekeeping," he leaned, touching his forehead to hers. "I'm not asking for anything, Grace. Instead, I'm giving you what you need. Time, space, a place to find yourself and someone who believes in you."

"What can I give you, Brody? You give so much and never ask for anything in return."

He kissed the top of her head and then held her

close. "When you feel as though you have found what you're looking for, you can put that ring on your finger and know that I will love you forever. Let me be your husband and a father to that little girl."

"How long...?"

He shrugged. "As long as you need. Well, not too long because I don't want to grow old alone. I want to grow old with you. And if you get to the end of this journey and realize that you don't want a cowboy or this slow country life, just leave the ring on the chain and..."

She put a finger to his lips, stopping him. If he said another word she would cry.

"Don't."

He kissed her finger. "I'm leaving all of the options open. This chain doesn't bind you to me. It's just a promise. It's my way of saying I'm here when you're ready for a cowboy with baggage and more dreams than sense. If you're ever ready."

"I don't know, Brody."

"I do. I'm not going to hover over you or try to convince you to stay here. I'm not going to get in your way of finding your dreams. But I'll be here. That ring is my promise. I'll be here for you."

She wrapped her fingers around the ring but she didn't put it on. She held it tight in her hand and she stood on tiptoe to kiss the cowboy who had her heart in his hand, and she wondered if he knew that.

Brody held her close and then he let her go and walked out the door. "It's all up to you, Grace."

"Brody?"

He looked back, smiling as he walked backward down the sidewalk. "Yeah, Grace?"

"You might not mean to make life complicated, but you do. But I'm glad you're in my world."

His laughter floated back to her. "Yeah, I know."

Chapter Seventeen

March was about the best month to be alive, Brody thought. At least it was for a cowboy living in Texas Hill Country. The weather was perfect, wildflowers were blooming and other than a little morning stiffness, he felt pretty near to perfect.

If a little bit lonely.

He led a saddled gelding to the fence where a group of kids stood waiting for him. They ranged in age from seven to twelve. There were four of them and they had recently been placed in a foster home. The youngest refused to talk. The oldest had some anger, justifiably so. Their dad had randomly beaten them and sometimes made them sleep in a shed. It was one of those stories that people didn't believe when they heard it on the news. But looking at these kids, at their eyes, it was written there for anyone to see who cared to take a closer look.

"This is Earl Grey." He introduced the gelding. "He loves kids."

"I don't like horses," Miss Twelve and Angry said.

Brody shrugged it off. "That's okay, Angie. He likes

you and, after you get to know him, you might change your mind."

"Doubtful," she muttered.

The littlest, a girl of seven, reached to pet the horse. The nine-year-old twins did the same. Miss Twelve and Angry crossed her arms in front of her and refused to look at her young siblings having fun. He guessed if she looked, she'd be tempted to join in, and she didn't want to give an inch.

He handed out carrots to the younger kids and tossed one Angie's way. She caught it, shooting him a glare in the process. If looks could kill...

A car came up the drive. He hadn't seen that car in more than a month. Not since she'd given birth to Bria. He watched her park, watched her get out. And then he put his focus back on the kids. They had first dibs after all.

Grace had left just days after having her baby girl. Her parents had come home from South America to be with her.

"Hey, he took my carrot." Angie reached to stroke Earl's jaw. "He isn't too bad."

"No, he isn't," Brody agreed. "Maybe next week you'll spend some time brushing him."

"When do we get to ride?" she asked, still petting the horse and actually warming up to the animal. Earl leaned in to the attention, soaking it up.

"You have to learn to take care of him first."

"Can he be the horse I ride?" she pushed. He let her because at least it was a response.

He had a dozen horses now. For the first couple of weeks, he'd just use Earl with these kids, letting them get used to this one horse. Soon he'd introduce them to the other animals. But Earl seemed to be a genius when it came to working with troubled kids.

Brody enjoyed working with them, too. It wasn't too many years back that he had been one of them.

"Well?" the girl asked again.

"I think I can arrange for you to ride him if you start participating."

She wrinkled her nose at him. "Fine."

"But you won't like it?" he teased.

She nearly laughed, but not quite.

The kids hugged him before they left, hurrying to the car where their foster mom waited. She waved as she got out to make sure they all got in and buckled.

And then Grace was there, standing in front of him. Bria was curled up warm and soft against her neck, a light blanket thrown over her. Brody reached and Grace shifted her daughter and placed her in his arms. He held the baby close, taking in her perfect face, her tiny nose and her dark eyes as she blinked awake, yawning and almost giving him a smile.

He fell in love. He'd probably walk on coals for that little girl. He'd definitely hurt anyone who tried to hurt her. Or her mother.

He shifted his gaze to Grace. He took in her smile, the way her brown eyes flickered with warmth and humor, the way just being near her righted his pretty crazy world.

"It's been a while." He spoke softly because Bria's eyes had closed again.

"I should have called." She bit down on her bottom lip and looked up at him. "I'm sorry."

"No need to be. I've been busy here, getting the riding camp off the ground. I have a dozen kids enrolled."

"That's amazing. I'm so proud of you, and so happy for the kids who will get to come here."

He shrugged off the compliment. Right now he didn't want to talk about him. He wanted to talk about her, about the baby and how they were doing.

"Let's go inside and have something cold to drink." He shifted the baby to his shoulder and headed toward the house. "Unless you have to go?"

"No, I don't have anywhere I have to be."

They walked side by side toward the house. He'd managed to make it feel like his home, this house of Lawton and Elizabeth's. He led Grace through the back door and down a hall to the kitchen.

"This is a little bigger than your trailer," she observed. Rather than taking the baby, she poured them both a glass of tea.

"Yeah, just a little. I'm getting used to it."

"I'm sure it took time."

Sally barked from the utility room. "I need to let her out."

Grace down set her glass. "Let me get her."

She returned, holding his dog. The Maltese licked her face, tail wagging.

"I guess my dog missed you, too."

She put Sally down. "I'm here to talk about that."

"About my dog missing you?" Brody sat at the island, still holding the baby, who didn't weigh much more than a bag of flour. She stretched and curled into his chest.

"Yes, I missed your dog," Grace said, taking him by surprise.

He chuckled, but then quieted, rubbing Bria's back when the baby grew restless. Grace stepped close and he fought the urge to wrap his free arm around her and pull her to him. It wouldn't be difficult, to hold them both. But he was still waiting, still wondering what had brought her here today.

"Really?" He spoke softly. "You leave town for a month and you missed a dog?"

"Yeah, I missed your dog," she teased. "And I missed Duke's chocolate cream pie. And my apartment at Oregon's. Among other things. But I managed to tie up some loose ends in my life while I was gone."

"I can't believe I'm jealous of chocolate cream pie." He leaned toward her. Man, she smelled good. "I've missed a few things, too."

"Did you?"

He took a deep breath and leaned away from her, letting the moment between them evaporate. He couldn't let her tangle up his thoughts to the point that he didn't know what he was doing. He had to get back on firm ground.

"So what loose ends did you tie up while you were in Fort Worth?"

"Finishing college, and adding psychology to my degree."

"I'm sure that will open up a lot of jobs."

"It might. But I'm thinking about becoming a nurse practitioner. Dad said there are options for getting a small clinic."

Now she had his attention. He eased the baby to his other shoulder and waited. Because he knew how to be patient.

Grace took the baby from his arms. He looked like a man who might forget he was holding an infant. "Let me go put her on the couch. Where is the couch?"

"There's a baby bed, if you want to put her down."

"That would be good. She might sleep a little longer in a bed."

He led her to a bedroom fit for a princess. Or twin princesses. It obviously had been the room Rosie and Violet had shared when they were infants. The cribs were white with multicolored quilts. The walls were the palest yellow. Brody pulled a soft blanket out of a drawer, and as she placed Bria in the crib he hovered nearby.

She'd never thought of him as the hovering type, but there he was, looming, watching, looking worried. She'd noticed the same malady in her dad and granddad. The minute the baby entered their lives they hovered, worried and overprotective.

"Will she be okay here?"

She smiled up at him. "She'll be fine. But there's a monitor. I'll take that with me."

Together they walked out of the room and down the hall to the living room. She walked immediately to the big windows that overlooked the fields, now filled with wildflowers. In the distance the hills were hazy as rain swept in from the south.

"It's beautiful here," she observed, knowing Brody stood close behind her.

"Yes, it is beautiful."

She turned into his embrace. With a tentative hand she brushed her fingers through his hair, She'd missed his presence, missed touching him. It came back, the fullness in her heart, the way he made her feel complete. No amount of degrees, no job, no community could do for her what he did.

"Brody, I'm here to stay."

"I was hoping."

He pulled her close, kissing near her temple, then tracing a path to her lips. Their mouths melded. She kissed him back, needing that moment with him. She'd missed him so much. She'd missed being in his arms. She'd missed the way he made her laugh, made her smile. She should tell him those things. Soon.

"You made a promise last winter," she reminded him.

"Did I?" His mouth quirked and she took the opportunity to place a kiss on his dimple.

"Yes, you did. You gave me a promise, and you gave me this." She pulled the chain off her neck and placed it in her hand, the ring with it. "You said when I'm ready."

"Yes, that's what I said." He took it, held it in his clenched fist.

"Brody, I'm ready. I want to wear that ring. I want to be in your life and I want you in our lives. I needed to have my baby and figure out what came next. What comes next is us. We should have come first, but I lost myself along the way and I didn't know who I was or what I wanted. I want us."

"I want us, too," he finally said, his voice raspy with emotion. "I've wanted us since forever."

He worked at the clasp on the chain and she took it from him and unhooked it. With fingers that trembled she slid the ring off the chain that had been keeping it close to her heart for the past few months.

Brody took the ring from her and held it in the light.

"I remember when I bought this. It was the shiniest, prettiest thing I'd ever seen, and I couldn't wait to put it on your finger. But you're wrong, Grace. We shouldn't have come first. God had to come first in this plan of ours. And neither of us got that. He will always be the center of our lives together, holding us on a firm foundation, making us the couple and the parents we need to be."

He slid the ring on her finger, a perfect fit. It twinkled in the soft lamplight of the living room. He turned her hand over, kissed her palm, then he wrapped her in his arms.

"Marry me, Grace Thomas. Let me be the husband you deserve and a father to your daughter."

"Yes, Brody. I'll marry you."

Their lips and their hearts met, and Grace knew what it meant to come home. She knew what had been missing since forever. She clung to Brody's shoulders.

A tiny cry over the monitor interrupted the moment. Brody smiled into the kiss and pulled away. He rested his forehead against hers and she held tight until her legs found strength again. The baby cried again, just a mewling sound.

"That's called divine intervention." He stepped back, letting her go.

They walked down the hallway to the room where sunshine streamed in the window and a baby girl waved her tiny hand, searching for her mommy. Brody lifted Bria from that crib and Grace felt the rightness in that moment and in the gesture. It had taken them a while to get here, to each other, to this place. But hadn't God always known?

"I love you, Bria Thomas." Brody kissed her baby's cheek, then he reached for Grace and she stepped into the circle of his arms. "And I sure do love your mom."

Epilogue

Grace stood in the vestibule of Martin's Crossing Community Church. She peeked through the doors that were closed so that her entrance would be special. It would be special, all right. As a mom, she knew the faint cries of her daughter, drifting back through the church. Bria was with her granny, but she had just sounded the dinner bell, wanting her mommy.

Grace's dad patted the hand on his arm. "Your mom can handle this."

"I know she can."

She watched as her new sisters walked down the aisle as bridesmaids. Oregon first with Duke, Jake with Breezy, and Samantha had informed them all she would walk herself down the aisle. So there wasn't a third groomsman. She'd learned that Sam did what Sam wanted, no matter how her brothers tried to control her. In that way she was very much like the half sister just eighteen months her junior. Kayla wasn't at the wedding. She'd taken a plane out of the country, just to annoy her dad.

"You're up, sunshine," her dad said with a slight

catch in the words. She looked up and caught the tear that trickled down his cheek.

"Daddy, you don't have to cry."

"Of course I do. My little girl is getting married today. You're going to leave your mother and me, and you're going to be a wife to Brody Martin. I like that young man, but I'm entrusting to him one of my most valuable possessions, something I cherish, my daughter."

"Now you're going to make me cry."

He kissed the top of her head. "Don't cry. But do be happy, Gracie. Be content. Be a woman of faith who raises her children to have faith."

"I'll do my best."

"That's all any of us can do. And never go to bed angry. Talk things out."

"Got it," she whispered, because the music had stopped. "Dad, they're waiting. Could you write this all down for me?"

"I'll send it in a text. With a note to Brody. He's a good man, Grace. You're both young and you will make mistakes. You'll get angry. But you'll work through those hard times if you keep God at the center of your marriage."

The wedding march started over again.

"I love you, Dad."

"I love you, Gracie." He hooked her hand over his arm and together they walked through the doors and down the center aisle of the church.

Grace focused on her goal, the man standing at the front of the church, seeking her, loving her. He smiled, revealing that dimple. His blue eyes captured hers, holding her steady on that walk to him.

"I love you, forever, Grace," he whispered as she stepped next to him.

Her dad gave her a quick hug and handed her over to Brody Martin. For richer or poorer, in sickness and in health. To love only him so long as they both might live.

"I love you, too." She held his hand, never wanting to let go.

The ceremony was short. The vows were sweet. And the kiss made the crowd cheer.

Brody grinned down at her. "Mrs. Brody Martin, let's go get our daughter."

Grace's mom stepped forward, handing them the four-month-old baby girl with blond hair and dark eyes like her mother. She had them both wrapped around her little finger. She cooed as if the whole ceremony had been all about her.

Brody held them close, and Grace knew that this was only the beginning.

* * * * *

Dear Reader,

Welcome back to Martin's Crossing. This cozy little town in Texas Hill Country is quickly becoming one of my favorite places. I'd love nothing more than a little house on the outskirts of town, a cup of tea with Mr. Mueller, or a Christmas ornament from Oregon's shop.

In *The Rancher's Second Chance*, you'll get to spend time with all of my favorite characters. I think you'll enjoy getting to know them all a little better. I think you'll definitely enjoy getting to know Brody Martin a little better. He's been hiding a few things, nursing a broken heart and trying to mend. That's all about to change.

Brenda Minton

REQUEST YOUR FREE BOOKS!

2 FREE INSPIRATIONAL NOVELS
PLUS 2
FREE
MYSTERY GIFTS

SPECIAL EXCERPT FROM

Love Inspired

*Will a young Amish widow's life change when her
brother-in-law arrives unexpectedly at her farm?*

Read on for a sneak preview of
THE AMISH MOTHER
The second book in the brand-new trilogy
LANCASTER COURTSHIPS

"You're living here with the children," Zack said. *"Alone?"*

"This is our home." Lizzie faced him, a petite woman
whose auburn hair suddenly appeared as if streaked with
various shades of reds under the autumn sun. Her vivid
green eyes and young, innocent face made her seem
vulnerable, but she must be a strong woman if she could
manage all seven of his nieces and nephews—and stand
defiantly before him as she was now without backing
down. He felt a glimmer of admiration for her.

"*Koom.* We're about to have our midday meal. Join us.
You must have come a long way." She bit her lip as she
briefly met his gaze.

Zack still couldn't believe that Abraham was dead. His
older brother had been only thirty-five years old. "What
happened to my *brooder*?"

Lizzie went pale. "He fell," she said in a choked voice,
"from the barn loft." He saw her hands clutch at the hem
of her apron. "He broke his neck and died instantly."

Zack felt shaken by the mental image. "I'm sorry. I
know it's hard." He, too, felt the loss. It hurt to realize that
he'd never see Abraham again.

"He was a *goot* man." She didn't look at him when she bent to pick up her basket, then straightened. "Are you coming in?" she asked as she finally met his gaze.

He nodded and then followed her as she started toward the house. He was surprised to see her uneven gait as she walked ahead of him, as if she'd injured her leg and limped because of the pain. "Lizzie, are *ya* hurt?" he asked compassionately.

She halted, then faced him with her chin tilted high, her eyes less than warm. "I'm not hurt," she said crisply. "I'm a cripple." And with that, she turned away and continued toward the house, leaving him to follow her.

Zack studied her back with mixed feelings. Concern. Worry. Uneasiness. He frowned as he watched her struggle to open the door. He stopped himself from helping, sensing that she wouldn't be pleased. Could a crippled, young nineteen-year-old woman raise a passel of *kinner* alone?

Don't miss
***THE AMISH MOTHER** by Rebecca Kertz,*
available October 2015 wherever
Love Inspired® books and ebooks are sold.

Clara turned, squatted and swept Libby into her arms.
"What would I do without my sweet girls?" She signaled
Eleanor to join them and hugged them both.

Blue turned away to hide the pain that must surely
envelop his face even as it claimed every corner of his
heart. That joy had been stolen from him, leaving him an
empty shell of a man.

The girls left their mother's arms and Libby caught
his hand. "Mr. Blue, did you see how full we got your
buckets?" She dragged him to the doorway where they'd
left the pails. Each one was packed hard with snow.
"Didn't we do good?"

"You did indeed."

She looked up at him with blue expectant eyes.

What did she want?

"Did we earn a hug?" she asked.

His insides froze then slowly melted with the warmth
of her trust. He bent over and hugged her then reached for

Eleanor who came readily to let him wrap his arm about her and pull her close.

Over the top of the girls' heads Clara's gaze pinned him back. She didn't need to say a word for him to hear her warning loud and clear. *Be careful with my children's affections.*

He had every intention of being careful. Not only with their affections but his own. That meant he must stop the talk and memories of his family. Must mind his own business when it came to questions about Clara's activities.

She could follow whatever course of action she chose.

So long as it didn't put her or the girls in danger, a little voice insisted. But he couldn't imagine she would ever do that.

He had no say in any of her choices whether or not they were risky. And that's just the way he wanted it.

Don't miss
A DADDY FOR CHRISTMAS
by Linda Ford,
available October 2015 wherever
Love Inspired® Historical books and ebooks are sold.

JUST CAN'T GET ENOUGH OF INSPIRATIONAL ROMANCE?

Join our social communities
and talk to us online!
You will have access to the latest
news on upcoming titles and special
promotions, but most important,
you can talk to other fans about your
favorite Love Inspired® reads.

 www.Facebook.com/LoveInspiredBooks

 www.Twitter.com/LoveInspiredBks

Harlequin.com/Community

LISOCIAL